Sarah, Sissy Weed and the Ships of the Desert

By Paula G. Paul

EAKIN PRESS
Austin, Texas

Library of Congress Cataloging in Publication Data

Paul, Paula G.
    Sissy weed and the ship of the desert.

    Summary: Sarah and R. J., residents of a small town on the Texas
coast in the 1850s, investigate whether the camels that have been
shipped to their town are really a front for some illegal cargo, such as
slaves.
        1. Children's stories, America. [1. Texas — Fiction]
I. Title.
PZ7.P27838Si   1985   [Fic]   85-3818
ISBN 0-89015-504-6

FIRST EDITION
Copyright © 1985
By Paula G. Paul

Published in the United States of America
By Eakin Press, P.O. Box 23066, Austin, Texas 78735

ISBN 0-89015-504-6

For my parents,
Frank and Sarah Griffith

Preface

Soon after the U.S. Army began importing camels to use as an experiment in transporting goods across the American desert, individuals began to import them for use in private business.

In the 1920s some people were still living who remembered the "widow's camels" brought into Indianola, Texas, and set loose because the widow who supposedly ordered them would not pay for them. A man named Chris Emmett interviewed those people to write his book *Texas Camel Tales* (published by Steck-Vaughn, San Antonio, Texas, copyright 1932, Austin, Texas, 1969). Some people thought the camels were a decoy for illegal slaves, and they said a man was found dead on the beach shortly after the slaves were unloaded.

Among the people who were interviewed by Mr. Emmett was Mrs. John Gonzales, whose husband, along with Joe Mendez, took charge of the "widow's camels." The character Mendez Gonzales in the book is based on those two men. Another man knew the real Hadji Ali, called Hi Jolly by Texans, who was in charge of the army's camels for Major Henry Wayne.

The slave auction described in the book is based on an actual description of such an auction in Galveston, Texas, in the mid-1800s.

Indianola was subject to storms similar to the one that Sarah McCluster encounters in the book and, in fact, was destroyed by a hurricane in 1875. There is nothing left of Indianola now but a few cemetery stones.

1.

Those beasts were wandering all over the town, near taking it over. Camels, they were.

Camels! All over Indianola, Texas.

It wasn't the first time I'd seen camels in our seaport at Indianola. The first boatload had docked here a little more than a year before. It was on April 29, 1856. But the United States Army was in charge then, and they certainly didn't set them free to roam the streets.

"What in the world is going on?" I asked R. J.

"Contraband," he said.

I might have known he'd say something like that. Just out of the blue. He's crazy sometimes. I didn't say a word; I just waited for him to ramble on.

"Mark my word, Sadie, there's contraband involved in this."

I hate it when he calls me "Sadie" and he knows it.

"My name is Sarah. Don't call me Sadie — and what do you mean by *contra* — ?"

He motioned for me to hush with a sweeping gesture of his hand and crept away, sort of on tiptoe, toward a young man standing a few feet away. I knew the man. Actually, he was more a boy than a man. He was Mendez

Gonzales, who works around the docks unloading cargo from ships that sail into our port. Mendez was talking to a sailor, and R. J. was eavesdropping on their conversation. I gave R. J. a disapproving look — but it was wasted. He was so absorbed with eavesdropping he didn't even notice it. He thought he was going to hear some deep, dark secret, no doubt.

R. J. is like that — got the wildest imagination you ever saw. And that imagination of his has gotten the best of him more than once. Take the time he claimed he saw the headless body of a woman in Powderhorn Bayou. It was right after a big storm swept in from the Gulf of Mexico.

He had the whole town stirred up with search parties out looking for the headless body. Oh yes, they found "her." It turned out to be Mrs. Fanny Adler's dressmaker's form. It was shaped big and buxom, just like Mrs. Adler, and it came in handy since she could fit dresses she was sewing onto the form instead of trying the dress on every time she sewed up a new seam. Dressmaker forms don't have legs or a head, of course, so when the storm caused floodwaters to rush into Mrs. Adler's house and wash away the things in her sewing room, the dress form really *did* look like a headless woman when R. J. saw it.

Of course I didn't see the dress form floating in the bayou myself, but I spent a lot of time explaining it to folk for R. J.'s sake. Somebody has to stand up for that crazy Frenchman, and since he's my best friend, it seems it has fallen upon my shoulders to do so.

Oh, I know people think it's odd that it's R. J. who's my best friend instead of a girl my own age. I'm twelve and R. J. is thirteen. And sure, I know every once in awhile someone who doesn't know us too well will think we're sweethearts just because we're "getting to that age," as they say. But the truth is, I've known R. J. since

2

I moved here with Mama and Papa. Six years ago I think it was. You can't be sweethearts with somebody you knew when they didn't have any front teeth.

Anyway, R. J. needs me. Somebody has to be his friend to help him out of those fixes he gets himself into with his imagination. And he thinks I need him to liven up my life a little. He thinks I'm too practical. I suspect he may also think I'm not very bright either. He probably thinks I don't know that contraband means illegal goods smuggled into a country.

And speaking of smuggling, R. J. got all excited about that once before too. There's a place about half a mile out of town called Smugglers' Cove. R. J. staked himself out there for two days and a night once. He claimed the cove didn't get its name for no reason at all, although nobody in town could remember why it was called that. But all he ever saw was the Widow Watson drive up in her buggy and meet someone. He seemed disappointed.

I told him maybe the Widow Watson was meeting a secret lover. That seemed pretty exciting to me, and I thought maybe it would cheer up R. J., but he wasn't interested. He had his heart set on smugglers. *He has his heart set on contraband this time,* I thought.

If he did, then I knew he was the one who wasn't too bright. Camels aren't contraband. They're perfectly legal. The U.S. Army has brought them in twice. As I said, the first time was a year ago. The officer in charge was a man named Major Wayne. He said the army was trying the camels out as beasts of burden in the desert country of Texas, and all the way across to California. Ships of the desert, he called them.

The army had also brought along some Arabs, Egyptians, and Turks to keep the camels in line, and to teach American soldiers how to handle them. Major Wayne

3

would have been shocked to see the beasts stampeding through the town the way they were now. Why, I just saw one chewing the top off of Miss Cassie Langstrom's fence post!

"My word, R. J., look at that critter!"

R. J. wasn't listening, so busy was he with his eavesdropping. That crazy Frenchman. R. J.'s full name is Robert Jules La Salle. He claims to be a descendant of Rene Robert Cavelier, Sieur de La Salle, the French explorer who landed here where Indianola is, back in 1685. I don't know whether to believe that or not. You never know about some of the things R. J. tells.

The camel chewing on Miss Cassie's fence turned around and rubbed its flank up against one of the short posts, the way a horse does when it has an itch that needs scratching. I had no doubt that the camel had an itch. I could tell, even from a distance of two blocks, that the camel was mangy. There were big bald patches on the critter's back where the hair had come out.

There was another mangy camel in the process of kneeling down right in the middle of Main Street, and two more were meandering over toward the mayor's house. The mayor's two black slaves were chucking rocks at them. A herd of about six looked like they were headed for the bayou. But the one in Miss Cassie's yard seemed to be causing the most trouble.

"R. J., I believe that camel is going to knock Miss Cassie's fence over — "

The white pickets were swaying like trees in a hurricane, and the camel just kept on rubbing. Then the fence sort of rippled like creek water when a snake slithers in, before part of it fell with a crash and a bounce.

After that, everything happened at once. Miss Cassie's front door slammed behind her as she stormed out onto her porch, and she let out a scream that could be

4

heard clear to Africa. The camel got one of its skinny legs caught between the pickets of the fence, and it commenced to kicking, trying to get it loose. That made the fence dance like the tail of a kite in the wind.

Miss Cassie screamed again, and all the people within hearing range started running toward her, including R. J. and me. At about that time, His Honor Mayor Andrew Seamore came riding through town on his fine Morgan horse.

I don't know if it was the dancing fence, Miss Cassie's screams, or the camel kicking in the middle of the street, but something spooked Mayor Seamore's horse. It reared and bucked, neighing with fright as it threw His Honor straight up in the air. Mayor Seamore lost his hat, and he landed on his bottom — but he was apparently unhurt, except for his dignity. His hat was in worse shape. It had landed right in the middle of a steaming pile of camel droppings.

I hadn't seen such goings on since Papa took me to a circus once in Galveston. R. J. was standing right beside me, and the sight of the mayor in a heap, with his hat in the manure, struck him as funny. He was literally shaking with laughter, and watching him laugh got me to laughing too. We were near about doubling over when I caught a glimpse of Mayor Seamore's face. He wasn't laughing, and the way his muttonchop whiskers were quivering, I knew he was angry.

Everyone was looking at us; everyone that is except Mendez and the sailor, who were busy freeing the camel's hoof from Miss Cassie's fence. Even Miss Cassie had stopped her screaming and was staring at us. It made me a mite uneasy.

"Come on R. J.," I said, sobering. "We best get home."

"*Sarah McCluster!*" Mayor Seamore said, before I

could get turned around and on my way. "Does your mother know where you are?" By this time he had helped himself up and was dusting his pinstripe trousers.

"Yes sir," I lied. It pains me to lie. It pains me even more to think how easy it comes to me sometimes, and me a Presbyterian. A minister's daughter, as a matter of fact.

"Are you sure of that?" the mayor persisted. "Most of the young ladies your age are in the charm and deportment class my wife teaches every Tuesday afternoon. Are you not a member of that class?"

"Yes, sir."

"Well?"

"Well, I — you see, Mama's not feeling well, and I wanted to get some flowers for her. I was going down by the bayou to gather them."

"The bayou is the opposite direction."

"Oh, well — you see, I — "

"And what's wrong with Mrs. McCluster?"

"Just the sniffles," I said. "Cholera," R. J. said at the same time.

Leave it to R. J. to come up with a more interesting ailment than I can. It did confuse His Honor, though. I could tell by the look on his face.

"It's just the sniffles, although it *seems* a little like cholera," I said, hoping to clear up the confusion.

It would have been much simpler if I could have just told him I'd skipped his wife's charm and deportment class because I hate it. But I didn't want to hurt his feelings. It's not his fault that I think all that walking with a book on your head is ridiculous. And learning which fork to use and the proper thing to say aren't much use to me.

The truth is, to my mind books are for reading, not balancing on your head, and we never have more than one fork to a plate anyway. As far as learning what is the proper things for young ladies to say, according to Mrs. Seamore, that's mostly nothing. "Young women of breeding should never be ostentatious in their show of knowledge, but rather should show interest in others," she always says. What she means is, girls should play dumb. I don't like that. I may be a little too practical, as R. J. says, but I'm not dumb.

I was beginning to feel that way now, though. I was getting myself into a corner with my lies. His Honor was giving me a suspicious look when R. J. came to my rescue.

"Come along, Sarah," he said. "We best get back to your Mama. She's expecting the flowers right away."

R. J. took me by the arm and began pulling me along. I turned around and smiled at Mayor Seamore. "I'll tell Mama you wish her well," I said.

By then the mayor paid me no mind. He was staring at his hat with a look of sadness.

R. J. kept jerking at my arm. Yet, instead of pulling me toward the bayou where the wild flowers grow, he was steering me back toward the wharf, mumbling something about contraband again.

"R. J., will you stop all this silliness," I said, yanking my arm from his grasp. R. J. may be older than I am, but he's an inch shorter, and I have to admit I'm a mite heftier. There's no reason in the world for me to let him pull me around. "I'd best get home before Mama starts to wonder about me," I said.

"You can wait a little longer," R. J. insisted. "I want to hear more about this contraband, and I want you — "

"Contraband, my hatband! This is just more of your wild imagination! I've got to get home. You stay here and play at your spying if you want."

"I'm not playing, Sadie, I'm telling you I overheard that Arab over there . . ."

"Don't call me Sadie! And that Arab is Mendez Gon-

7

zales, and he's Mexican. I'll declare, R. J., don't you know an Arab from a Mexican?"

"If you weren't so dumb, you'd know that Mexicans have Arab blood in their veins because of the Moors in Spain," R. J. said in a superior tone. He wasn't about to be proven wrong by a girl.

"That's nice, R. J., that you think you know their genealogy." I was glad to have that word to throw at him. Call me dumb, will he?

Mrs. Seamore had just given us that word the week before. It has something to do with a family's ancestors. I tried to look just as superior as R. J. did when I said it, but it was hard with the wind pulling my hair loose from the braids and blowing it into my eyes.

Maybe if your hair is flaming red or jet black, you can look haughty and defiant when the wind blows, but mine's brown, almost the same color as my freckles. And besides blowing into my eyes, it was now blowing into my mouth, making me spit and sputter.

"I'm going home," I said, giving up on trying to look haughty and superior.

"No, Sarah, wait," R. J. said, running after me. "I need you to help me figure this out."

I stopped, but I didn't turn around. I knew what R. J. was doing. That little squirt of a Frenchman is good at sweet-talking me into things. He does it all the time. First he'll insult me, tell me I have no imagination or that I'm dull or too practical. Then when I'm good and mad, he'll use flattery and tell me he needs my practical viewpoint or my good sense. I guess it would make me even madder if it weren't true. He really does need me to help level him out every once in awhile.

"Let me figure it out for you fast," I said, turning to face him. "Camels are not contraband. They're legal. So there is no mystery, except maybe why they turned them loose on the streets."

"I know the answer to that," R. J. said.

"Then *you* tell *me* why."

"Because whoever bought them refused to pay for them. That's what I overheard. They were brought here from the desert for some businessman — or something — this time, and not for the army."

"Oh, well then, it's probable that whoever bought them decided he didn't want them because they're so mangy. But that doesn't make them contraband," I said.

R. J. had a sad and disappointed look on his face, like I'd solved his mystery for him, and it had turned out to be dull and practical after all.

"You think that's it?"

"Most likely."

"You don't think the camels were a decoy, maybe — to smuggle something else in — like *guns* maybe?" He brightened a little at the possibility.

"Guns for who? Or what?"

"For . . . well, I don't know . . ."

"Come along, R. J.," I said, taking his arm this time. "Come with me to explain to Mama where I've been. She'll want to know about the excitement the camels have caused."

We walked away from the wharf and started toward my house. We met Mendez and the sailor on their way back to the wharf after rescuing the camel from Miss Cassie's fence, and as we passed, I spoke to them.

"Those critters are making a mess of this town," I said. "You really shouldn't have turned them loose like that."

"It's not our fault, Senorita," Mendez said. "We tried to find someone to buy them, or at least feed them."

"That's right, Miss," the sailor said. "The lady who

9

ordered them wouldn't pay, and the captain doesn't seem to care. It's strange that he doesn't even care that he didn't get his money. All he can think of is pulling out to-night. He won't even take on food and water. All I can say is, I'm glad I only signed up for one trip with him."

"Who ordered the camels? Who is it who won't pay?" R. J. asked, edging closer to the two men. He was like a detective closing in.

"It was a Señora Watson. A widow, I think," Mendez answered.

I didn't have to look at R. J. I knew without looking he'd have that gleam in his eye.

R. J. was so excited his feet hardly hit the ground as he walked along with me to my house.

"You hear that?" he asked. "The Widow Watson. I told you there was something to that meeting she had at Smugglers' Cove. It's contraband. I know it! Gold maybe. Or silver."

"R. J., you're not making sense. Why would anyone smuggle in gold or silver?"

"Because they're valuable."

"But nobody would have to smuggle it. A lot of ships bring it in legally."

"Sadie, you're so full of good sense, you're blinded to the truth. I tell you, there's something exciting going on here, and I aim to find out what."

"Good for you. Be sure and let me know when you've solved the mystery," I said, walking ahead of him. I hate it when he gets uppity.

As I glanced toward our house, I saw Mama standing on the front porch. She had her hands on her hips, and I could tell she had one of those I'm-not-happy-with-you looks on her face.

"Well, I'll be seeing you later," R. J. said. "I'm going

11

to study on this mystery for awhile and figure out my next move."

I knew by that he'd seen the look on Mama's face too. Since he had already turned around and was headed for his house over on the next street, there was nothing for me to do but go face Mama alone.

"Hello, Mama," I said in my most cheerful voice.

"Young lady, I'm not happy with you."

It turned out that Mrs. Seamore had sent one of the girls by the house during the refreshment break to inquire if I was ill.

"You can imagine my surprise at her question, and my embarrassment when I realized that you must have skipped the class," Mama said.

"I'm sorry to concern or embarrass you, Mama. I truly am, but you see I was on my way to charm and deportment class after school when I saw a ship in the harbor. I thought I'd just have a look before class, but I met R. J. on the wharf. And, would you believe it? There were camels on the ship!"

"You've seen camels before. All those the army kept in the government corrals — "

"Yes, but they turned these critters loose. They aren't government camels."

"Turned them loose?"

"One of 'em took a bite out of Miss Cassie's fence, then knocked it down scratchin' its itch."

"Upon my word!"

"And the mayor's horse threw him when it reared from fright at one of 'em."

She brought both her hands to cover her mouth and sucked in her breath. "You don't say," she said. "And was he hurt?"

"No, but his hat will never be the same."

"Oh, does your father know?" she asked. "I must

12

make sure he does," she said before I could answer her. "Miss Cassie is bound to be upset and will need comforting." She was off the front steps and hurrying next door to the church where Papa would be in his study, preparing his sermon.

I was off the hook for awhile, at least, and by the time I saw Papa walking into the house, I knew he had convinced Mama to go easy on me.

"It isn't every day a herd of camels chews up fences and parades up and down the streets," he said to me.

"No, it isn't, Papa."

"So it's natural you'd want to watch the excitement."

"You're so right, Papa." Papa doesn't like disagreements, and he goes to great lengths to understand both sides so as to keep trouble down.

"But still, you need to learn to do what's expected of you. It was expected that you would attend Mrs. Seamore's charm and deportment class after school."

"Yes, Papa."

"I hope you understand that it's only because this kind of excitement doesn't happen every day that I'm letting it go this time. Just don't let it happen again."

"I understand, Papa."

Mama was shaking her head. She thinks Papa's not strict enough, but all she said was, "I only hope today's class didn't touch on something important you'll be expected to display in your conduct at the soiree tonight."

I had forgotten all about the soiree. That's what Mrs. Seamore calls her little gatherings she has from time to time to give us girls a chance to practice our charming manners. A soiree is kind of like a party, only dull, and usually you're expected to dance. It's at times like this I wish I'd been born a Baptist. They don't hold with dancing. But, at least I'd learned to pronounce it "*swä-ray*," in French.

13

Later that evening, as I was helping Mama with supper and still feeling sorry for myself for having to go to the soiree, she sent me out to the garden for some fresh radishes. That's when I saw R. J. again.

"Hey, Sadie," he said, walking up to the back fence. "What do you say we take a walk up to the widow's place?"

"No, thanks," I said, "and my name's Sarah."

"I'd like to figure out what's going on. Wouldn't you?"

"Snooping around other people's property is bad manners," I told him. "Besides, I'm helping Mama with supper."

"How about after supper?"

"I have to go to Mrs. Seamore's soiree."

"Can't you sneak away?"

I gave R. J. a look that would wither a whole field full of radishes. I was skating on thin ice because of what I'd already done, and I wasn't about to let the ice get thinner. R. J. took the hint. He shrugged his shoulders and walked away.

"Who was that I heard you talking to in the back?" Mama asked later, at supper.

"It was R. J."

Mama heaved a sigh and turned her blue-green gaze on Papa, but she was still talking to me. "I'll declare, you do spend a lot of time with R. J.," she said. "I'd have thought you'd have outgrown that tomboy stage by now and started to act like a young lady."

"Don't rush her into growing up," Papa said, cutting his meat into tiny pieces. "Besides, R. J. is a nice Christian boy."

"He's Catholic," Mama said, heaping a spoonful of green beans on Papa's plate.

"We're all God's children, Louise."

14

That night, I squeezed into the dress Mama had made for me to wear to the soirees. It was muslin, printed with tiny blue flowers and a blue ribbon sash to match, but it was a tight squeeze. I must have gotten two inches thicker around all my parts since the last time I had worn it.

I had to walk kind of stiff-like all the way to the Seamores' to keep from ripping the seams. That made it seem a much longer walk than the five blocks it is.

The Seamores have the grandest house in town, although not nearly as grand as the planters' homes up in Brazoria and Colorado Counties. But the Seamores do have a veranda all around and a parlor big enough to hold a string band for the soirees. There's a chandelier in each of the downstairs rooms, and a winding cherrywood staircase leading to the rooms upstairs. The kitchen is out in back, away from the main house. The Seamores' is also the only house in town with a bathtub and a chamber pot built right in.

Besides that, it's the only house where there are slaves to run it. Some of the farmers farther inland own one or two slaves, but I never knew anyone who owned them until the Seamores bought the two they own. They are Bella, the cook and house servant, and Jimmy, who works in the yard and sometimes helps out in the house. Folks say the Brazoria County planters would call that just plain tacky, since they all own forty or fifty blacks for their plantations.

Just the two the Seamores own have been enough to cause Papa some concern, though. He has said privately to Mama and me several times that one human being ought not to own another. It grieves him that the country has only gotten as far as making it illegal to bring new slaves in from Africa or other countries, and hasn't stopped slavery altogether.

But slavery is a subject that gets folks riled up, so the only thing Papa's ever says publicly in a sermon is that we're all God's children, black and white. Folks don't seem to mind that, as long as neither God nor Papa interferes with which child owns another child. Like I said, Papa doesn't like disagreements, so he does his best to keep things peaceable.

So do I, most of the time. That's why I was trying to be on my best behavior at the soiree and not let on that I was bored. Besides, if I made a fool of myself by pouting or being anything except charming, Mama would make me go through Mrs. Seamore's school all over again, and I just couldn't stand the thought of that.

I acted interested in people's conversations without showing off my own knowledge, even though Willie Barlow made the most ridiculous brag about how he could catch catfish in the bayou using minnows for bait, when I knew full well I could catch just as many with worms. When the time came to drink punch, I held the cup with just the tips of my fingers, and I even danced a waltz with Willie.

He only asked me, of course, because his mama made him, and if knowing that wasn't misery enough for me, he couldn't keep his feet off my toes. About the third time he stepped on them, I was swearing an oath I'd be a Baptist before the next soiree rolled around. But the dance finally ended, and to calm myself, I took a little pastry from the tray Bella brought around.

She looked a mite tired, I thought, and she didn't smile at me the way she usually does. That concerned me some, since I like Bella a lot, and I know she likes me, too. She's been my salvation more than once in charm and deportment class by signaling to me which fork to use or when I wasn't holding my teacup just right — things like that.

16

"What's the matter, Bella? You look kind of peaked," I said.

"Ain't fittin' you be talkin' to the help, Miss Sarah. You go on an' practice your social graces on the white folks."

"Bella . . ."

"Go on. I'm powerful tired anyhow. Miz Seamore's got me cookin' an' servin' an' cleanin'. I'm powerful tired."

Bella went off toward the kitchen still grumbling to herself. I looked around and saw Mrs. Seamore in her shiny dark blue satiny dress, giving instructions to the bandmaster. Mrs. Seamore's dress seemed to fit a bit tight around the middle, like the seams were about to pop, but it isn't polite to notice things like that. I tried looking at her hair instead. It was parted in the middle with ringlets over her ears. Her hair is dark brown, but the funny greenish tint it has to it makes me think she uses hair dye. It's not polite to notice that either, so I concentrated on the pastry I was eating.

About that time, the string band the Seamores had hired from Galveston, struck up a tune for a fast dance called the Schottische. By all that was right and holy, I shouldn't have had to dance that one. Willie Barlow had done his duty by asking me once, and since I'm not the raving beauty Lilly Downs, the grocer's daughter is, there wouldn't be anybody standing in line to ask me now. Their mamas would make them go on to the wallflower who had been sitting the longest, and I'd get a rest.

I had just watched Lilly Downs whirl past in her white dimity gown with the pink flounces on the bottom when I felt a hand on my shoulder. I figured it was Willie Barlow asking me to dance just to torment me.

"Get your hands off me or I'll bust your lip!" I said.

17

It's hard to be charming when your feet hurt and your dress is squeezing the life out of you.

"You're a sweet-talking thing, certain for sure," says my would-be partner. It was R. J. I was only mildly surprised to see him there. We have a shortage of boys in town, and R. J. is often called upon by Mrs. Seamore and cajoled by his mother to do his duty and show up at the dances. Mrs. La Salle does not come. I doubt that she's invited since she has to take in ironing and sell vegetables to support herself, her being a widow. Mrs. Seamore seems to think a woman who supports herself is not fitting.

R. J. grabbed me by the forearm and pulled me out onto the floor. Now R. J. is not the world's best dancer, but I'd never seen him do so poorly before.

"You're out of step," I said, glad that at least I didn't have to be charming and pretend he was perfect.

"It ain't me," he said. "Trying to dance with you is like dancing with a herd of camels." R. J. doesn't worry about being charming either.

"What are you trying to do? Run me square into the wall?"

"The door, Sadie. Dance toward the door."

"Don't call me Sadie — *Ouch!*"

He near took the skin off my elbow swooping me through the door.

"What's this all about," I asked, rubbing my elbow.

"Shhh," R. J. said, pointing toward a couple in the shadows. I recognized Lilly Downs's pink and white flounces. It looked like she was kissing somebody in the dark.

R. J. kept pulling me until we were around the corner of the mayor's house and headed for the street.

"Where are we going?" I asked.

"The widow's house."

18

"Oh no, we're not," I said, stopping right where I was.

"Listen to me," R. J. pleaded. "I saw the captain of the vessel that unloaded the camels headed up that way as I was on my way to the Seamores'."

"So what? Maybe he's a suitor."

"But that's not all. I *know* there's something in the hold of that ship the camels were on."

"So what?"

"Something alive."

"More camels? Maybe the sick ones are down in the hold."

"No, I heard a sound. Like a human cry."

I could feel a chill down my back. *A human being in the hold of the ship? But who? I wondered. A prisoner? A madman? And what did the Widow Watson have to do with it?*

I knew, even as I did so, that I was going to regret following R. J. up the hill to the widow's house.

The night around us was a gauzy gray and webbed with moonlight and moonshadows, making a person see things that weren't there. And, I feared, *not* see things that *were* there.

The widow's house was on the edge of town and about a hundred yards up a hill from the beach. We could see a light in the parlor window long before we reached the house. The tiny yellow glow seemed only to make the night more eerie.

As we drew nearer, R. J. put a finger to his lips, signaling for me to be quiet. I could see that R. J. was about to walk all the way up to the window, and I was in no mind to do that. There was trouble here, no doubt about it. If there was a human being in the hold of the ship — a prisoner of the widow or captain — I wasn't *about* to do anything that would provoke them to throw me in there, too. It was only logical to think that way.

But it was R. J. La Salle, no logical thinking boy, who had got me as far up the hill as I was. It was R. J. who took me by the arm and pulled me near off my feet, dragging me all the way up to the window. I may be a preacher's daughter, but that kind of rough treatment

20

makes me angry enough to hit that Frenchman square in the mouth with my fist and swear at him to boot. It was the necessity of remaining undetected, not my religion, that kept me from doing it.

Once we were up close to the window, we kept our heads down low. We could hear the murmur of voices coming from the inside, and I could tell that one was a man's voice, and one a woman's. Curiosity got the best of me so that I even managed to forget how mad I was at R. J. I was the first to be brave enough to raise my head so that my eyes were just above the window ledge, allowing me to see what was going on inside.

Sure enough, there was the widow and a man dressed like a ship's captain in dark blue woolen breeches and a coat with two rows of brass buttons down the front. The captain was a swarthy man with a chiseled face and deep-set eyes. The widow was fair-skinned and gray-eyed and tall for a woman, almost as tall as the captain. I'd seen her before, of course, around town. She hadn't lived in Indianola more than four or five months, and nobody knew her very well — they just knew she was a widow.

The lamp with the stingy yellow light was on the table between them, and there were some papers strewn around the tabletop. The widow and the captain seemed to be arguing about something.

"I tell you, woman, it's too big a risk," I heard the captain say, "and I'm not for risking my life by getting caught."

"How can you get caught?" the widow asked him. "Nobody ever goes to the cove at night."

"I just want to make sure of that," the captain answered. Then I heard him say something about "scout around," but I wasn't sure exactly what he said, because it was just about then that R. J. bumped his chin on the window ledge. It was just a little thud, but it was enough

21

to startle the captain and the Widow Watson. They both got up and started for the window. R. J. and I took off running as fast as we could into a clump of trees a few yards away.

"They were talking about the cove," R. J. said in a hoarse whisper.

"*Shhh*," I said, fearful that the widow and the captain would hear him. But R. J. just wouldn't shut up.

"Do you suppose they mean Smugglers' Cove?" he asked.

I shrugged my shoulders, afraid to say anything. But R. J. knew the answer to his own question. It was the only cove in the area.

"They're going to unload the contraband there. That's what they were talking about," R. J. whispered.

I pulled R. J. back farther into the woods, where I was pretty sure the captain and the widow wouldn't find us. "R. J., do you suppose if they unload the contraband, they'll unload the person too? And I was just thinking, suppose he's a madman. Suppose he's a crew member who went mad and they put him down there."

"Who?" R. J. asked.

"The person you said you heard in the hold of the ship. Human sounds you said."

"But I didn't know it was a madman. Who told you that?"

"Nobody. I was just wondering. I mean, why else would they keep someone hidden away like that?"

"Is the madman guarding the contraband?"

"I don't *know*, R. J. I don't even know if there *is* a madman. I just . . . Oh, never mind."

It's hard to get things through that Frenchman's head sometimes.

"I think we ought to go out to the cove," he said, which is exactly what I was afraid he was going to say.

"No, R. J."

"Why not?"

"We have no business out there, and besides I need to get back to Mrs. Seamore's soiree." I didn't add that I was scared. If he didn't know that, he didn't have the imagination I thought he had.

"It would take only a minute," R. J. said, being his most persistent. "We could just go see if they're going to unload the contraband tonight."

"We don't know that there is any contraband in the first place, and even if there is, it may not be unloaded tonight in the second place, and — "

"And in the third place," R. J. interrupted, "you want to know who the madman is as much as I do."

"Forget about the madman."

"I can't, and neither can you."

"There is no madman, R. J."

"Prove it. Come with me to the cove and see if they set him free or chain him to the contraband."

"No."

But it did no good to protest. R. J. had already started for Smugglers' Cove, and he knew I wasn't going to walk back to town in the dark by myself. I wasn't going to stay there alone in the night either.

It seemed even darker out by the cove, since there were no lights visible from the town. I kept stumbling over rocks and brush and looking back over my shoulder toward town, but R. J. just kept walking, and, of course, I followed him. The wind was also stronger out there, carrying the fish and salt smell of the seawater to us. Most of the time I enjoyed the smell of the bay and the gulf, but even that seemed menacing tonight.

"Let's go back," I said. "You can see there's nothing here." And I was right. There was nothing to see except the sand and the water, and in the distance, the lights of the ship that had unloaded the camels.

"Look," R. J. said, pointing toward the water. "There's a ship out there."

"Of course there is, silly. That's the one that unloaded the camels. It's anchored offshore."

"Oh," R. J. said, and I could hear the disappointment in his voice. He really wanted that ship to come around the cove and unload some contraband.

It occurred to me then that the ship had been docked in port that afternoon, and I couldn't imagine why it would have moved offshore and anchored again, but I didn't say anything to R. J. It's not a good idea to get his imagination stirred up. I kept watching the ship while R. J. nosed around the brush and out in the sand for some sign of contraband.

While I was watching, I saw a lanternlight, probably in a rowboat, get closer and closer to the ship. I figured it was the captain rowing out from shore after talking to the widow. I kept watching for several minutes, until R. J. came running back to me, all excited and out of breath.

"Sarah, come with me! I want to show you something. Over there!"

"What is it, R. J.?"

"Not what — *who*."

I ran with R. J. up a distance from the water's edge, and R. J. pointed toward a spot farther up that was strewn with large rocks. A campfire was burning near some of the rocks.

"There," he whispered. "There's somebody out there."

He was right. There was somebody out there. We could see someone in the light of the campfire, but I could see nothing to get excited about.

24

"That's just someone camping on the beach. People do that all the time. You know that. See his boat near the shore? He's probably fishing."

"Maybe he's got the contraband," R. J. said. "See that lump in the sand, over there by his campfire?"

"That lump is his bedroll, silly."

We both fell silent, watching the man for a moment. Sure enough, he went over to the lump and unrolled it, then lay down on the rolled out blankets.

"Sadie . . ."

"Don't call me Sadie."

"Do you think — "

"Do I think it could be the madman?"

I don't know what made me say that, knowing it would scare R. J. or get his wild imagination going, or both. But sometimes R. J. just invites me to torment him.

"Oh, Lordy," he said, and I could sense him shivering in the darkness.

I knew that was no madman out there, but just a fisherman. Still, what happened next got me to going for a minute, too. R. J. jumped near out of his skin, let out a yelp and ran out into the clearing in plain sight of the stranger. In almost the same instant, I felt something nudging at my back. I stole a glance over my shoulder, then I was following R. J., running as fast as I could.

We ran all the way back to town and up to the Seamores' place. I beat R. J. to the Seamores' door by a good ten minutes. Just as I skidded inside, I saw Mama coming out of the dining room. I could tell by the look on her face that she'd been looking for me, and that she was not pleased because she couldn't find me, so I grabbed the first human I could find and started waltzing. It just happened to be Willie Barlow.

"What in hell do you think you're doing, Sarah McCluster?"

"Waltzing, you fool, and watch your language, or I'll dance you straight into hell."

"You ain't dancer enough to do that."

"Don't make any smart alec remarks about my waltzing if you want to stay healthy."

"You waltz fine, but that's a schottische the band is playing."

I caught a glimpse of Mama staring at me with a funny look on her face. I smiled at her as nice as I could and tried to let Willie lead.

Just then, R. J. stumbled in the door. He went straight to the punch bowl and drank from the dipper, then he backed up to a chair and slid himself into it, looking wide-eyed as a minstrel player and scared as a goose over hunters.

I knew I'd have to work my way over to him in a little while and tell him the thing that crept up on us out at the cove was no madman, as I knew he feared, but one of the loose camels. I'd seen that when the thing nudged me, and I had looked back over my shoulder. I hadn't wanted to tell R. J. it was only a camel. I had not wanted to lose out on the best chance I'd had to get him out of there. And I did want him out of there. There was something strange going on. I could just feel it.

I f it hadn't been for the dead man over on Powderhorn
Bayou, I would have been questioned about my long
disappearance from Mrs. Seamore's party.

As it was, Mama was too upset about the dead man
to remember to ask me about the soiree. We learned
about the dead man when Abel Duncan, the sheriff, came
to our door about daybreak the morning after the party.
He came to get Papa. They always get a "man of the
cloth," as they say, when somebody dies.

Sheriff Duncan's knock at the door woke me up, and
I stood at the top of the stairs listening as he talked to
Papa. I overheard him say that it was he who had found
the man. Sheriff Duncan lives out by the bayou, and he
said he got up before daylight to chase the stray camels
away from his garden.

"Didn't want the malformed creatures stompin' my
peas and eatin' my corn," he said. He told Papa he chased
the camels all the way to the banks of the bayou, and
that's when he saw the man, stone cold dead, with no papers to identify him anywhere on his person.

I saw Mama's pretty seashell pink face turn as white
as chalk, and she looked like she was going to faint. She

went right back to bed with a damp cloth folded across her forehead, and that gave me the opportunity I wanted to follow Papa and Sheriff Duncan to the bayou.

Who would have thought there would already be a crowd down there, since Papa was supposedly one of the first to be notified? I surely didn't expect it, but there was a crowd all right, and I spotted R. J. right off.

"Have you seen the dead man yet?" I asked R. J., when I could work my way over to him.

"No, I haven't, but I heard he's not from Indianola. A stranger, they say."

"I heard that. Sheriff Duncan says he had no papers on him to identify him." It made me feel right important to have that message to pass along, even though I wasn't one of the first on the scene.

"Doc Teague says his death was caused by a blow to the head," R. J. said, not wanting me to be one up on him. "Come on," he said, "let's have a look."

He took my hand and we wormed our way through the crowd. When we got up near the front of the mass of people, we could see Doc Teague and the sheriff talking together and Papa leaning over the man, praying. R. J. and I both edged a little closer, but what we saw made us stop still in our tracks. My hand tightened around R. J.'s and I could feel his fingers grow cold. The dead man was the same man we had seen camping at Smugglers' Cove.

R. J. and I gave each other a look, but neither of us seemed able to speak. Just then the sheriff stepped forward and spoke to the crowd.

"Does anyone here recognize this man?" he asked.

I opened my mouth to speak, but nothing came out. It was like a thief had stolen my voice and replaced it with a wad of cotton in my throat. I heard R. J. make a funny weak sound, and I figured he was having the same trouble I was. The sound coming from the crowd was a

28

steady murmur, with everyone disavowing that he knew the stranger and wondering aloud who the man could be.

"We got to tell what we know," I managed to whisper to R. J.

R. J. nodded his head affirmatively, but still said nothing.

"All right folks," Sheriff Duncan said. "Let's break it up. You can all go home now, and we'll leave this to the undertaker."

As the townsfolk started to move away, R. J. walked up to Sheriff Duncan, and I followed right behind him.

"Excuse me, sir," R. J. said, pulling at the sheriff's sleeve. "I know a little something I think you should know."

"And what's that?" the sheriff asked, looking a little annoyed as well as suspicious.

"It's about the dead man. I've seen him before."

"Have you now!" Sheriff Duncan asked. I could tell by his tone of voice that he was remembering the headless woman in the bayou.

"He's telling the truth," I said. "I saw him, too. We both saw him."

"Sure you did," the sheriff said.

"But sir, it's true," R. J. insisted. "We saw this man when we were out by the cove looking for the madman."

"Looking for the what?" Sheriff Duncan asked, getting a funny look on his face.

"He said madman, only there wasn't one," I said, speaking up quickly, trying to come to R. J.'s defense before he made us both look like fools. But R. J. was bound and determined.

"No, we didn't see the madman," he said. "He may be in the hold, but there's contraband — "

The sheriff started laughing, making the bulge that hung over his belt bounce up and down like a cork bobbing in the water. "A madman!" he exclaimed. "And contraband!" He walked away, laughing so hard his face turned red.

"Well, I like that," I said, watching him go. "He should have listened. We might have given him a clue to help him solve this mystery."

"What kind of clue?"

"I don't know. Maybe he could have found one of his own, if he'd just go out to the cove where the man was camped. As it is, he didn't even give us the chance to say he *was* camped there."

"Nothing to stop us from looking around out there for clues."

"R. J.!"

"Well, what would it hurt?"

I was just about to give him a list when R. J. interrupted. He commenced to nagging me to meet him at the wharf after supper when he got all his chores done, so we could walk over to the cove and explore for clues. I told him I wasn't going to do it.

"You're crazier than a bedbug," I said, and I reminded him that the last man out on the cove had been killed by a blow to the head.

That didn't stop R. J. for a minute. You'd think it would. But it didn't. "This has got my curiosity up," he says, and he tells me how he's convinced it's all got something to do with the contraband. Well, in the end, I agreed to meet him. I just got to thinking it would be simpler to be there to try to keep him out of trouble than it would be to unravel later whatever he got himself into.

When I got home, I made no mention to Mama and Papa of the fact that I had seen the dead man out at the cove when he was still alive. I had no intention of keeping it from them forever, of course. It was just that if I told them right then, I knew they wouldn't let me out of the house to meet R. J. As it turned out, I had trouble anyway.

"Child, don't you know there was a dead man found out by the bayou this morning?" Mama said to me when I asked for permission to go see R. J. "I can't let you out of the house this late. The streets of Indianola are no longer safe for children."

"There's no need to worry. A dead man can't hurt me, Mama."

"It's not the dead man I'm worried about. It's who may have done the deed."

Of course, I knew that was what she was getting at. I was just trying to divert her attention.

"I'm sure we'll be safe, Mama. Especially since there'll be two of us. I'll be with R. J."

"R. J.!" she said, throwing up her hands. "Sarah, you're getting to be a young lady. Playing with boys is so, well, *unseemly*. I was hoping you'd form a fast friendship with someone in your charm and deportment classes and start acting like a lady."

Mama's mission in life is to turn me into a lady. I did not want to get her started on that, so I excused myself and went to my room, feeling pretty sure R. J. would be by before long, looking for me. Sure enough, it wasn't fifteen minutes before he was tossing pebbles at my window. I raised the window and leaned my head out.

"Mama says I can't go out."

"Why not?"

"Because of the dead man."

"What about the dead man?"

"Mama thinks whoever killed him might be roaming the streets."

"Oh," said R. J., as if the thought hadn't occurred to him before. He glanced uneasily over his shoulder. "I was

FRANK SMITH, JR. LIBRARY CENTER
SOUTHWESTERN UNIVERSITY
GEORGETOWN, TEXAS 78626

3 3053 00237 1516

thinking maybe it was safe, now that the madman is gone," he said.

"What madman?"

"The one you said was in the ship."

He was at it again! "I didn't say there was a madman in the ship," I said pronouncing my words slowly, so maybe he'd get it this time. "I only said — oh, never mind that. What do you mean the madman is gone?"

"Well, the ship is gone anyway."

"What?"

"I saw it sailing out of the harbor. Out that way." He pointed in the direction of the cove.

"Do you suppose that ship has something to do with the dead man?" I asked in a whisper.

"Speak up, Sarah, I can't hear you," R. J. called from down below.

I tried whispering louder. "I said . . . Oh, heck," I said aloud. "Turn around and look the other way."

"What?"

"I said turn around and look the other way. I have to hitch up my skirt to climb out this window."

R. J. did as I said, and I climbed out the window and scooted across the roof of the verandah to the porch railing and climbed down it like a ladder. I had done it many times before when I took a notion to look at the stars or to listen to the distant sound of the gulf waters. By climbing down the porch railing, I didn't have to worry about waking up Mama and Papa when I walked through the hall.

I'd never done it before to slip away, though. It seemed dishonest. Papa was always lamenting what he calls "the blighted record of Presbyterian honesty," and I sure hated to add to the blight. At the moment, however, I couldn't think of a good enough reason not to.

Just outside the gate, R. J. stopped still in his tracks, staring at something ahead of him. I saw the huge dark

mass, too, and it startled me for a moment. We both realized at almost the same instant that it was another one of
the stray camels munching on the prairie grass outside of
our fence.

The creature kneeled down on its front legs, staying
that way a moment, as if it were praying for us. Then it
settled down on its haunches and chewed contentedly,
giving us a long look as we passed by.

I got a picture in my mind, of myself, riding one of
the beasts along the beach at night — on the African
coast — with seven gossamer veils flowing out from my
body in the breeze, and a train of admirers on camels behind me. I vowed right then and there, I'd have a ride on
one of those critters before long.

R. J. was strangely quiet all the way to the cove. The
crazy Frenchman was probably still thinking about the
madman. When we were almost there, he stopped and
pointed at something in front of us. It was the ship, anchored just a little way offshore in the cove. She was a
ghostly sight, with her sails reefed and her mast and rig-
gings looking like a spiney skeleton in the moonlight.
Her dark hull was creaking and bobbing in the inky
waters.

"Her name's *Glory Star,*" R. J. whispered.

Listening carefully, we could hear voices coming
from the vessel. I motioned for R. J. to stay quiet, while
we tried to hide ourselves in the brush. It was a needless
gesture, as he was too frightened to speak anyway.

Suddenly, we were both surprised to hear a splash,
and judging from what we could make out by the lanternlight coming from the ship and the pale moonlight re-
flecting on the water, it appeared that someone had
jumped from the side of the ship and was attempting to
swim to shore. In just a little while, we heard another

splash, and another and another. It wasn't long before we saw people wading to the beach.

It wasn't so dark that I couldn't make out that they were all Negroes. I would say there were about ten in all, and some of them were women and children. Presently, a white man rowed to shore in a dinghy and said something to them in a strange language, and then he separated himself from them, moving to a small bluff where he built a campfire.

When lanternlight appeared on a ridge above him, he got up and walked toward it. I could tell the person carrying the lantern was a woman, and as near as I could make out, it was the Widow Watson. I couldn't tell what she and the man were saying, but I figured the campfire must have been a signal to her, and I had figured out what was happening.

"There's your contraband," I whispered to R. J.

R. J. looked at me with a question in his eyes.

"Slaves," I whispered.

He nodded his head yes, to show he understood. These slaves were fresh from Africa, and that made them illegal contraband. They wouldn't be illegal, of course, if they had been born to slavery in the U.S. Some say it will take a war to stop that.

As we watched, the blacks started to mill around, talking among themselves while the white man was up on the ridge with the woman. The men in the crowd kept glancing nervously toward the *Glory Star,* making me think maybe guns were trained on them.

I realized then why the camper R. J. and I had seen on the beach was killed. He must have found out about the slaves. Maybe the crew had tried to unload them earlier. Anyway, it was for certain the captain and his crew couldn't risk anyone finding out about their illegal contraband. They could be imprisoned for slave running.

That meant R. J. and I were in danger, too, and we had to get away from there before we were seen.

At just that moment, I saw a small child, a baby really, stray from the crowd and toddle toward the brush where R. J. and I were hiding. Someone darted out, chasing the baby, and I was afraid to move, afraid it would attract attention.

The person chasing the baby was a girl. I could tell that as she drew nearer. She was bare from her waist up, and her breasts were beginning to develop just as mine were. She got closer and closer to our hiding place until suddenly her eyes met mine and then moved to take in R. J. She stood there awhile, staring at both of us, showing more surprise at seeing us than shame at her half-naked body. I thought for a moment she was going to scream and give us away, but she picked up the child and ran back to the group.

Now someone knew that we knew about the contraband. Would the fact that it was one of the slaves who knew, protect us?

I turned to look at R. J., and the expression on his face told me he was just as frightened as I was. In fact, he was too scared to be embarrassed or surprised at the girl's nakedness.

"She saw us!" I whispered.

"Let's get out of here!" R. J. said. He had already started through the brush, headed back toward town.

I followed right behind him, and we both ran as hard as we could until we got to my front yard. We sat there, waiting for our breath to catch up with us and listening to our hearts beat like the jungle drum from Africa I'd heard a missionary play once.

"Well, at least we know what the contraband is," I said. It was all I could think of to say, and it seemed we needed something to fill up the silence besides the thumping of our hearts.

R. J. didn't respond, and the silence was making me uneasy, so I spoke again.

"That explains the voices too. It was slaves, not a madman."

R. J. stared straight ahead like a deaf mute, but that

Frenchman can't fool me. I knew what he was thinking, so I said it for him.

"Somebody killed the stranger we saw camped on the beach because he saw what we saw."

"If that slave girl tells anybody she saw us, we could be killed, too," R. J. said in a strange voice, as if he were just coming out of a trance.

"She's just a slave," I said. "Why would she want to tell? Besides, if she's new from Africa, she probably can't speak English."

"We'll just hope that's true," R. J. said.

But I could tell he was afraid it wasn't true. No telling what an imagination like his could conjure up — maybe the possibility that someone else could have seen us as well. Or that the slave girl could let it slip, without meaning to, that she had seen us. It's a good thing I'm not encumbered with an imagination that can dream up things like that, because just guessing at R. J.'s imaginings was making me fretful. I decided it was time I went back in the house.

"You going to be all right going home by yourself?" I asked, getting ready to climb the porch railing.

"Sure," he said.

"You're not too scared?"

"Naw."

I knew he was lying by the way he lingered, and by the way he made a move as if to follow me to the porch railing before he turned and walked up the street. I would have walked him home if I could have, but I knew I dared not take the time. As it was, I barely made it back to my room before Papa stuck his head in to tell me good night.

I had committed the sin of deceit, I knew, and worry about it kept me awake for close to ten minutes.

The next day I had a notion to run over to R. J.'s

house and try to work out a way to tell somebody what we had seen and to get them to believe it. But I didn't, the reason being socks and underwear. Mama had me mending them. Lordy how I hate the task! Needles seem to develop minds of their own once they're in my hands.

I was doing battle with a nickel-plated size six that had an eye no bigger than a freckle on a flea when Lilly Downs stopped by to visit. Mama said it was "delightful" that I had a chance to visit with another young lady instead of playing tomboy games with R. J.

Lilly is not a bad sort, and I usually don't mind talking with her even though she is beautiful and smaller than all the boys. She always knows what all the latest news is from Galveston, since her papa travels there all the time to buy goods to stock his store, and she gets to go with him. On this particular day, though, I was having a hard time concentrating on what she was saying.

"You ought to have seen the dress I saw this lady wearing in the Tremont House Hotel. It was cut down to here," she said, pointing to the middle of her chest. "You'd have thought she ran out of material. But there were yards and yards of material in the skirt. Fifteen flounces! I counted them. *Fifteen*. What do you think of that?"

"Amazing." I couldn't help thinking of the African girl I'd seen, naked except for a loincloth.

"Sarah!" Lilly said in a little while, startling me. "I said, do you know what the new sleeves are called?"

"Of course I do."

"No you don't. They're called *engageantes*. That's a French word. It means undersleeve. Sarah, are you listening to me?"

"Yes. You said she wore fifteen loincloths."

"Sarah!"

"Er . . . sleeves. Fifteen undersleeves."

38

I'm afraid I'd said something to upset Lilly. She left in a huff. I was truly sorry, but I didn't dwell on it much. I was still thinking about that slave girl, and I knew R. J. and I should try again to tell someone about seeing the dead man on the beach before he was a dead man, and about the slaves as well. We just had to make sure we wouldn't end up like the dead man if we talked.

Since it was already getting on toward night, I knew I'd have to wait until the next day, which was Sunday, to talk to R. J., and it would have to be after church. R. J., I knew, would go to early mass and be out by nine o'clock, but Presbyterians drag on until noon.

For once I didn't mind though. It would give me more time to think. In fact, I was hoping Papa would tie into one of his long-winded sermons on the evils of strong drink or gambling or bearing false witness or not giving enough in the collection plate or some other sin that takes a lot of haranguing.

As it turned out, he didn't. In spite of the fact that the church was full, with His Honor and Mrs. Seamore right on the front row, Papa lit right into a virtue instead of a sin, and everybody knows that doesn't take as long. He preached his brotherly love sermon — the one where he says we're all God's children, black and white — and he cut it so short Mama's pot roast wasn't even done when he got through.

I reasoned that Mama needed my help fixing dinner, and when I offered my help, she felt my forehead to see if I had a fever. She accepted my offer, though, and got a concerned look on her face when I said I'd do the dishes all by myself.

"Are you sure you're all right?" she asked.

"Of course, I am, Mama. I'm a young lady now. Don't be surprised if I show concern and responsibility and a willingness to help quite often now."

Mama gave me a funny look and asked if maybe I had a stomachache. I assured her I was fine, and then I managed to putter around cleaning the kitchen until the middle of the afternoon. Also, it occurred to me that I hadn't read aloud to Mama in some time. Jane Austin and the Bronte sisters are her favorites, but since it was Sunday, I had to read the *Bible,* of course. I read from the book of Second Samuel and from First Kings all about King David, but Mama made me skip over the parts about Bathsheba. That made reading a bit tiresome, so I had to take a nap.

The fact is, I managed to wile away the whole day without going over to talk to R. J., and I noticed he was making himself scarce around my house too. I was bound to see him on Monday, though, and we'd make some kind of decision then.

As luck would have it, I didn't see R. J. on Monday. His mama told me, when I finally got around to going to his house, that he had a cold in his chest. He was sick all week. The last time he was sick a week was during school in the winter. He missed several exercises in mental arithmetic, a paper on long division, conjugation of irregular verbs, and the Norman Conquest. This time he only missed the camel that got its foot hung in one of the low swings the school authorities had put up in the schoolyard for the little kids.

Getting its foot hung like that must have made the beast mad, because when Willie Barlow walked up to it, showing off how he wasn't afraid, it spit at him. Willie screamed like he'd been shot, because he'd heard that camel spit is poison. He thought his arm would fall off from the elbow down, since that was where the spit hit him. It didn't fall off, but it kept us all wondering about it every day, and that kept my mind off the slaves and off my conscience. At least a little.

I guess there had been enough worry over my conscience, and about the slaves, and the dead man, to show on me anyway, judging from what I heard Mama telling Papa one night.

"Seeing the dead man must have upset her, Bill," she said. "I should have warned her not to go down there."

"She'll be fine. She's a strong girl," Papa said, in that way he has of always denying anything is wrong.

"But she's so pale and listless," Mama insisted. "She's just not herself."

"Maybe a little trip would do her good," Papa suggested. "I'll take her with me when I go to Galveston for the committee."

"You do that, Bill, you do that," I heard Mama say. "It will be good for her. In fact, let's make it a family outing."

Ordinarily I would have been glad to hear we were going to Galveston, but not this time. Going to Galveston wouldn't help me solve my problem, and it was getting worse. The longer I waited to tell anyone about the slaves, the harder it seemed to tell it. Still, when Papa asked me if I wanted to go, I tried to sound pleased.

"Of course I want to go, Papa."

"A change of scene will do you good," he said, "and the committee is giving us the opportunity we need."

"What's the committee?" I asked.

"The mayor's Camel Committee," said Papa. "Since he has pressing business matters of his own, he has appointed a group of us to decide what must be done about the beasts, and the committee has asked me to see the commander of the army unit in Galveston to ask him to take charge of these stray beasts that are all over our town. Someone said they belonged to the Widow Watson, but she'll make no claim to them. She told me herself she didn't order them. So now, I reckon it's up to the town to get rid of them."

41

"You've talked to the Widow Watson?"

"Yes, as chairman of the committee, I — "

"At her house?"

"Of course, I . . . Sarah, you're being a mite saucy, interrupting me with your questions."

"Sorry, Papa."

He was right, I guess. I was being a mite saucy. But it did interest me powerfully to think of Papa climbing the hill to the widow's house and sitting down and talking to that tall, black-frocked woman. What had she done with the Africans while she talked to Papa? Surely he would mention it if they'd been there. But then, maybe not. Sometimes Papa is blinded to things that seem the most obvious.

I couldn't be cheerful when it came time to leave for Galveston Thursday, but I at least tried not to be gloomy, so as not to upset Mama and Papa. When I learned we'd be traveling up the Gulf Coast by ship, my spirits did lift some. I love sailing.

We got passage on a cargo ship, a square-rigger named the *Elissa*. She was a beautiful sight from the shore, with her sails as white as Mama's sheets on wash-day, but once on board, it was plain to see she was not a fancy ship. Even the little bit of teakwood she did sport looked weathered, and in need of varnishing. But no one seemed to mind, it being such a pleasant day for a sail.

At first I enjoyed sitting on the benches on the poop deck, feeling the breeze on my face and watching the gulls. Then Mama and Papa got into a discussion with another passenger about whether or not slavery should be legal in the Western territories, and I began to get restless. Papa was saying for the third time that we are all God's children black and white, when I decided I'd have a look around the ship.

I hadn't gone far along the rocking, swaying deck when I saw a passageway leading downward, and I began to wonder what it would be like to be held prisoner in the hold of such a ship. It seemed a shame not to try to find out while I had the opportunity, so I started down the ladder in the passageway.

As soon as I got myself turned around straight, I found myself in a crowded space, dark except for the light of a weak lantern, and full of unpleasant human body smells. I saw several sailors lounging around on bunks, some with no shirts on, and drinking what I'm sure must have been rum. You'd have thought the men were raving lunatics the way they carried on when they saw me.

If they'd only given me a chance I could have set their minds at ease. Let them know that I wasn't even the littlest bit shocked to see such a sight, since a preacher's daughter is quite accustomed to sin, having heard so much about it . . . and so often. They didn't give me the chance, though, and I never made it down to the hold. One of the sailors, a surly sort of fellow, ordered me above.

By the time I got back to Mama and Papa, they had shifted the conversation to the subject of unpredictable weather, and how turkeys can drown in a rainstorm. It was of no interest to me, so I passed the time as best I could, forming pictures in my mind of the hold of a ship where it's dark and damp and where rats scurry across your feet. After awhile it got to be downright nerve-racking, and I was mighty glad when at last I saw the outline of Galveston Island, and the wharves and piers jutting out into the green water.

The first thing we had to do after we docked was hurry over to the Tremont House and get a room for our stay. Such an extravagance is not common for a preacher's family, but the committee was helping with the expenses. I knew I ought to do my best to enjoy it, and by the time I finished my bread pudding with burnt sugar topping that was served to us for dessert, I was beginning to get the hang of it.

The next day, Papa was a bit reluctant to leave Mama and me alone in such a place as Galveston, while he went to see the army. Mama put an end to his worrying.

"You go on, Bill," she said. "The mayor made you chairman of the committee, and he's counting on you. Sarah and I will be perfectly content to rest awhile in our room, then maybe we'll have a look in some of the shops along the boardwalk."

I would not be content with resting. I would be bored, but of course I didn't say that aloud. *Why, I wondered, didn't I bring a book along to read?* All was not lost, though. As we walked through the lobby of the hotel, I spied a newspaper someone had left on one of the leather sofas. I picked it up and took it to the room with me.

"Look, Mama, I've found a paper. Shall I read to you?" I asked. She had already removed her suit jacket and was loosening her collar.

"If you like," she said, bending to unlace her boots before she made herself comfortable on the big feather bed.

I gave the paper a sharp snap and settled down to read aloud. A NEAR DISASTER, the headline said.

> We received word last week of John Bundy being hit by a train in Houston. We are told he failed to spur his horse fast enough as he crossed the tracks. But the train moved slowly, giving both man and beast a slight bump. John Bundy fell from his horse and has a broken leg. Fortunately, it was not the horse, as he would have had to be shot.

I looked up in time to see the funny look on Mama's face. It must be that she didn't like hearing of such close calls, I decided, so I read her an account of Elizabeth Menard's engagement party. Mama doesn't know Elizabeth Menard from Adam's rib, but the story did seem to

45

relax her some. In fact, by the time I finished it, she was snoring softly.

I was just about to toss the paper aside when an advertisement on the back page caught my eye. It was headed,

AUCTION HELD ON SATURDAY.
Bidders are welcome to view the stock ahead of time, beginning at two o'clock at the auction block near Pier Six. Included will be several strong bucks as well as kitchen maids and field hands.

I was reading about a slave auction! *Would it be nearby?* There were piers within walking distance of the hotel, I knew. Was Pier Six one of the ones we had passed on our way up? Well it wouldn't do for me to be wondering about things like that. I tried to sit quietly and let Mama sleep.

I grew more and more restless, and I couldn't seem to stop pacing the room. Without really meaning to do it, I found myself walking down the stairs, through the lobby, and out of the hotel.

Orleanders lined the streets with rosy colors and fragrance, and there was a faint smell of the sea. I tried not to think of the sea or of the piers that jutted into the gulf. Instead, I kept my head turned toward store windows and the front doors of houses built close to the street. Before long, I heard the noise of a crowd coming from across the street. I turned my head and saw that several people had gathered at one of the piers.

There were both black people and white people in the group, as well as people of all shades in between. There were elegant ladies in lace-trimmed gowns and slender men in pants of soft wool. Some of the blacks were elegantly dressed and some were in shabby dress. Because it was such an interesting crowd, I crossed the street for a closer look. That's when I saw a large platform and two white men standing on it. One was nicely dressed in a

46

waistcoat, which is a vest, and fancy shirt, while the other was in work clothes. Behind the platform were Negroes, standing in rows. I knew without a doubt that I had *stumbled* upon Pier Six.

I crossed the street to have a better look, and as I watched, a well-dressed white man from the crowd approached the line of Negroes and beckoned one of them to step forward. The Negro man he had summoned was then made to open his mouth for the white man to inspect, as if he were inspecting the mouth of a horse. Then he led the Negro man behind a wooden screen, and I heard another man in the crowd explain to the lady beside him that the slaves were led behind the screen to strip their clothes for further inspection. I wondered if, had there not been white women in the crowd, the slave women would have been subjected to the same inspection.

Just then a hush came over the crowd, and I looked up to see the white man in the waistcoat raising his hands to get the full attention of everyone.

"Ladies and gentlemen," he said when all was quiet. "The slaves that I have now to sell are the property of several masters. One of the gentleman has fallen upon hard times and must part with some of his property to pay his debts. And you can be assured that none of the slaves are being sold because they are not good slaves, but because of hard necessity."

He signaled for one of the black men to come forward to stand beside him. "Ladies and gentlemen, here is a strong, healthy, able-bodied buck," he said. "You could nowhere find a better hand for field work. What am I bid for him?"

"Eight hundred dollars," a man in the crowd shouted, and the woman beside him clasped her hands together and nearly swooned from excitement.

The auctioneer began a singsong, asking for numbers and pointing his finger from one to another of those in the crowd. I began to catch some of the excitement myself, feeling giddy and lightheaded as I watched. The black man was finally sold for twelve hundred dollars, and a woman in a gray dress was brought forward.

I watched her face as the auctioneer spoke of her good disposition and her ability to take care of a house. She stared straight ahead all the while, as if her eyes were fixed on something in another world. Then when the bidding started, she dropped her eyes for the shame of it. She sold for four hundred dollars, and when the hammer sounded, signaling the final bid, she spoke for the first time.

"Massah," she said, addressing the man who had just bought her. "Beg pardon, but if you buy my child, my Janey, she make you a good kitchen maid. You never be sorry you buy either of us."

"Where is she?" the man asked.

The woman pointed to a girl in the row of slaves. The little girl looked back at her mother, frightened as a rabbit.

"How old is she?" The white master asked.

"Eight, Massah."

"Looks scrawny for eight."

"Oh, that's 'cause she don't eat much, but she's strong, and she's trained good."

"Ummm. We shall see — if the bidding is not set too high," the white master said.

I saw the look that passed between the girl and her mother as the white man led the mother away to sign the papers for the purchase.

"A buck of about twenty," I heard the auctioneer say. "Strong and young. Could be trained as a field hand or to work with livestock. What am I bid?"

"Fresh from Africa, I'd wager," I heard a man next to me say.

48

"Can't be," the young man next to him said. "New stock is illegal."

"Oh they're not illegal once the ship's captain sells them to a broker," the older man said. "If there's a bill of sale they can't technically be called new stock. Lots of ways to get around the law you know," he said with a laugh.

The man sold for considerably less than the man before him, and another woman was brought out next. She looked to be about Mama's age, and as she stepped to the platform, a small child in the line of Negroes behind the platform reached his arms toward her. The woman uttered a little cry.

"Quiet that bellowing wench," the auctioneer said to the man in work clothes, who gave the woman a shove. As he did so, the woman fell to her knees.

I turned away, unable to watch anymore. I only wanted to get back to the hotel and Mama, and away from the ugliness of what I had just seen. But the little one cried out again, and I glanced once more toward the rows of Negroes waiting to be auctioned. Someone picked up the baby and held him, trying to comfort him. It was the girl I had seen at Smugglers Cove!

As I watched, I saw someone walk up to her and force her, even as she held the crying child, to open her mouth for inspection. The man doing the inspection was His Honor Mayor Seamore. Standing a few steps away, behind the row of Negroes was the Widow Watson. Mayor Seamore hadn't seen me, but the widow had!

I managed to get back to the hotel room before Mama awoke from her nap. She didn't even know that I'd been gone.

I was very upset because of what I'd seen, but I couldn't say anything. If I did, I'd be in trouble for leaving the hotel room alone without permission. It's powerful hard not to talk about things that are weighing heavy on your mind.

I tried not to let it show that I was so troubled, but Mama must have guessed something. She kept asking me why I wasn't eating much supper, but I didn't have to say anything because Papa said it was because I'd eaten too much bread pudding with burnt sugar topping the day before. That seemed to satisfy her.

Papa told us later during supper that he had arranged for the army to pick up the camels that were menacing Indianola. He said they would send an Arab ahead of the soldiers to round up the beasts. We wouldn't be leaving right away, he said, because he wanted to make arrangements with a shipping firm to have some hymnbooks shipped to Galveston from Scotland.

"The herdsman should be in Indianola before we are.

The army won't be there until several days later, but it could be that Indianola's camel menace will be ended by the end of the month," Papa said.

I tried to concentrate on having our town back to normal again, hoping the thought would soothe me. But it didn't. I didn't sleep much that night. I just tossed and turned in the little bed the hotel people had set up beside the big bed Mama and Papa slept in. I kept them awake some too. Papa laid my restlessness onto the fact that I wasn't used to sleeping in a hotel.

I wanted to shout out loud that it was because I didn't know if the girl named Janey got bought by the same man who bought her mama. It was because I kept worrying about the African girl and because I kept wondering about what His Honor Mayor Seamore was up to that I didn't sleep. The mayor had told Papa business would keep him from going with him to settle the camel problem. Well, it was business all right, but *bad* business, I feared.

I didn't shout anything out loud. I just kept it to myself all during the two days we stayed in Galveston, as well as the third day when we sailed back to Indianola.

We had to get back that day, it being a Saturday and Papa with a sermon to preach on Sunday. We got back late on Saturday, and I noticed right away that the slave ship was gone. I didn't have a chance to see R. J. until after church the next day.

But before that, something happened in church that so shocked me it near sent me into a swoon. Papa's sermon was on the sins of a prideful nature, and since I had heard more or less the same thing before, and since I myself am not troubled with a prideful nature anyway, I got to fidgeting. Just as his sermon was stretching on to half past twelve, I happened to glance over my shoulder as I shifted about, and whom should I see in the pew behind me and slightly to my right but the Widow Watson! I got the distinct feeling that she was watching me, and hadn't heard a word about the sins of a prideful nature.

I feared for sure that she was going to stop me after church, and I did my best to avoid her. However, before I knew it she was standing beside me on the front lawn.

"I hope you enjoyed your stay in Galveston," she said.

"Yes, thank you," I said in a weak voice.

"I hope you live to enjoy many more visits to Galveston," she said with a cold smile, then she walked away.

I kept telling myself she was just being polite, but I couldn't make myself believe it. I decided that if I could talk to R. J. about it I'd feel better.

It took some doing to find R. J., though. When I knocked on his door, his mother answered and told me he'd had gone with some other boys out to the bayou. I rushed right out there and saw the cluster of boys as I approached. I also saw right away that R. J. wasn't among them.

"Has anybody seen R. J.?" I asked as soon as I was near enough for them to hear.

They all turned around and stared at me, as if I had just escaped from a leper colony.

"What are you doing here?" Jason Fugue asked. Boys can act so high and mighty sometimes it gives me a pain.

"I just told you; I'm looking for R. J.," I said.

"Well, he ain't here. We ain't seen him at all today," Jason said.

I could tell by the way he looked that he was lying to me, and I didn't even know Jason was Presbyterian.

"His Mama said he was here," I said.

"His Mama said!" Willie Barlow said in a mocking

tone. "Well, his Mama must be mistaken, and you'd better get home. This ain't no soiree. Girls ain't welcome."

It wasn't anything I wasn't used to. I'd been in situations before where "girls ain't welcome." I figured they'd been fishing in the bayou. They all knew I was a better fisherman than any of them, and they just didn't want me showing them up.

All of a sudden it hit me that there wasn't a fishing pole in sight. It had to be something else. Just then I heard R. J. yelling, and I turned around and saw him riding toward me on a camel!

An Arab was leading the camel around by a rope, and Mendez was walking along beside the Arab. I knew the first man was an Arab by his headdress. It was like those worn by the Arabs the army had brought along before to help with the camels. He was wearing trousers like any other man in Texas might wear, and since his swarthy face looked very much like Mendez's, it was only his headdress that distinguished him as Arabian. He had to be the Arab — the one Papa had said the army had sent us to round up the beasts. Now I knew why the boys had wanted to get rid of me. They wanted all the camel riding time to themselves.

When Major Henry Wayne had been in charge of the Army's camels last year, riding them had been strictly forbidden. But if the rules were relaxed now that the Arabs were in charge, no bunch of boys was going to beat me out of something I'd wanted for a whole year.

At first though, I was too astonished to say anything about it. R. J. was such a sight sitting in that funny looking basket they use for a camel saddle! He would have reminded a person of an Arabian Sheik perched up there if he hadn't had on his old pants with the patch on the knee.

"R. J.!" I called, running toward him when I finally got my wits about me.

The Arab held up his hand, motioning for me to stop. "Missy, don't frighten the he cimmel," he said.

I watched as he tapped the camel's knees with a long pole to coax it to kneel so R. J. could climb off the beast's back. What fun it would be to ride high up on the camel's hump like that, feeling the swaying motion of a ship of the desert.

"This here is Hi Jolly," R. J. said after he had climbed out of the basket. He pointed to the Arab as he spoke. "He's teaching Mendez how to handle camels, so Mendez can help him round 'em up for the army."

The Arab wasn't much taller than I am, and his desert-brown face and dark eyes looked young in spite of the thick drooping mustache that framed his smile.

"I'm Miss Sarah McCluster," I said, since R. J. had forgotten to mention it.

The Arab greeted me with a low sweeping bow.

"What was your name again?" I asked.

A strange foreign word flipped off his tongue, and I squinted at him wondering what it was.

"I will write for Missy," he said, squatting to mark with his finger in the damp sand around the bayou. He stood and pointed to where he had written, "Hadji Ali."

"Hi Jolly," R. J. said.

The Arab shrugged slightly and repeated, "Hi Jolly," as if he had decided that was close enough.

"How do you do, Hi Jolly," I said.

"Hi Jolly is the best camel trainer in Texas," R. J. said.

"Hadji Ali is best cimmel man in the whole world," Hi Jolly said, making a wide sweep with his arm when he said "world."

"Oh, pardon me. The whole world," R. J. said.

"But I am a cimmel man. Not a magic genie. I cannot make world's second best cimmel man out of a mere Mexican in two weeks as Major Vernon in Galveston says I must." He gave Mendez a disgusted look as he said that, and it was clear it made Mendez angry.

"What do you mean by mere Mexican? I am not mere. I am of a proud family in Mexico, descendants of *conquistadores* whose roots I can trace for generations back to Spain. I'm betting you can't trace yours to your father!"

Now that made Hi Jolly mad, and he spat fire at Mendez in a foreign tongue.

"Don't swear at me in your godless language!" Mendez shouted.

"Then what language do you wish?" Hi Jolly asked, his swarthy face growing purple with rage. "I am a man of many languages, and I know the vilest oaths of all. Would you like the language of the black man in Africa? He has a word for a certain part of the monkey's body that would suit you well!"

Mendez drew back to take a swinging punch at Hi Jolly, and would have hit him I'm certain, had I not stepped between them. "I see you are giving the boys rides on the camels," I said, "and as a matter of fact, I have long wanted a ride myself. I wonder if you would allow me to —"

"Hey! You can't do that. It's my turn," Willie said, stepping in front of me. "I've been waiting all morning."

"Yeah," Jason said. "It's Willie's turn. Besides, a girl can't ride a camel."

Now that made me mad. I turned around to tell him *this* girl can do anything she sets her mind to, which is more than I can say for some boys. It was just on the tip of my tongue to spit out, but I thought better of it.

"Why Jason, I wouldn't dream of taking Willie's turn. You go right ahead, Willie," I said in a sugary sweet voice.

Jason and Willie both gave me a funny look, like they couldn't figure out what I was up to. I knew they'd never guess that I just wanted to watch how it was done, so I wouldn't make a fool of myself when my turn came up. Just because I'd been wanting to ride a camel ever since I'd seen the first one off the ship in Indianola the year before, didn't mean I had the slightest notion how to keep from falling off.

Hi Jolly got the camel to kneel again, and I noticed that the basket saddle was scooped out in the middle to cradle the rider. He helped Willie climb into the saddle, and I noticed Willie got jostled around from side to side as the camel stood up, but he managed to stay in the saddle by hanging onto the pommel. I knew I could do that too.

"Missy will ride the cimmel next," Hi Jolly said with a definite nod of his head.

I nodded back, thinking, *You bet your buttons I will.* I would ride like an infidel princess fleeing from some dreadful sheik who wanted to sell me into bondage for heaven knows what purpose. I could almost hear the old sheik shouting as I fled from him on my trusty camel.

"Stop! Stop this minute. What in tarnation do you young rascals think you're doing?"

It wasn't a wicked sheik I saw when I turned, but His Honor. He was winded and lathered when he stopped in front of us.

"I want to know what you think you're doing with that camel?" He asked, gasping for breath.

All of the boys just stood there looking like scared rabbits and not saying a word. The mayor's face got redder and redder.

"We're just riding one of the he cimmels . . . er . . . camels," I said, thinking *somebody* better say something before His Honor exploded.

"That's what I heard you were doing," Mayor Seamore said. He was so angry he was sort of dancing around, like somebody standing barefoot on hot sand. "I can't allow that," he said.

"But why not?" I asked, not meaning to sound impertinent. I was just wondering what rights the mayor had to have a say about camels that didn't belong to him.

His Honor looked a bit troubled by my question. "Why, because . . . because it's dangerous. Yes of course. It's dangerous. If those creatures will eat trees and fences, no telling what they'll do to humans."

"It's all right. We have Hi Jolly here helping us," I said, pointing to the Arab. "The army sent him here to help us. He's a trained camel driver."

"Yes, yes," the mayor said. "He was Major Wayne's camel driver, I'm told. And because of that, he should know better than to risk lives. And you should know better too, Sarah McCluster. You should know that riding camels is not ladylike. Haven't you learned anything in Mrs. Seamore's charm and deportment classes?"

He turned and surveyed the group of boys before I could think of a suitable answer. "All of you go on home," he said, pushing his hands at us as if he might be shooing away flies.

"I'll deal with you later," he said, looking at Hi Jolly. "And if that camel is damaged in any way that keeps the army from buying him, I'll deal with you for certain."

So that's it, I thought. It was more the safety of the camel he was concerned with than the safety of the boys and me. And he was concerned about the camel because of the money it would bring. Of course, the money was *supposed* to go into the town treasury, not to the mayor. But His Honor always did have a strong interest in the treasury.

"Come on," I said, turning to R. J. "It looks like I'm

not going to get my ride on a camel just yet, but I've got something important to talk to you about anyway."

"And boy do I have something to tell you," R. J. said.

I was just about to insist that R. J. let me tell him first when I heard Willie Barlow's voice taunting. "I'll bet it was you who snitched," he said looking straight at me.

"It wasn't me, Willie," I said impatiently. He had an ornery look on his face, but I was in no mood to tangle with him. I had other things on my mind.

"It had to be you," Willie insisted. "The mayor showed up right after you did. You led him to us, and it's for sure snitchin' ain't ladylike. Do you have classes in how to snitch at Mrs. Seamore's? I'll bet you're the star pupil."

Everybody except R. J. laughed when Willie said that, and it sure made me angry. But I did my best to hold my tongue and my temper. All I said was, "Don't be ridiculous, Willie."

"Bet you did snitch," said Jason.

"Sure she did," Willie said. "She's tryin' to get on the good side of the mayor so's he'll fill her pa's collection plate."

Willie was getting on my nerves, and I had to clamp my teeth together to keep from telling him off.

"Your pa don't ever do nothin' to make the mayor mad, does he?" Willie said. "Everybody knows he don't like them slaves the mayor has, but he dare not say a word against them. He'd have the mayor and everybody else down on him then, wouldn't he? And there wouldn't be nothin' in the collection plate. Your pa sent you to spy on us for the mayor, didn't he?"

Before I could stop myself, I hit Willie Barlow square in the nose. The blood squirted from it like a fountain. Willie just looked kind of surprised, then wiped at his

58

nose with the back of his hand. He yelped like a puppy when he saw the red.

It didn't take a fortune-teller to know what would happen next. Word would get back to Mama and Papa about me and Willie's nose, and I'd be confined to my room every day for at least a week. No telling when I'd get to talk to R. J.

"Let's get out of here," I said, grabbing R. J.'s hand. "I got to talk to you, and I got to talk fast."

We hurried away, but the boys followed us, taunting and singing,

Sarah McCluster, Nose Buster.
Sarah McCluster, Nose Buster.

It was mighty grating on my nerves. I was sorely tempted to live up to the name they gave me and bust a few *more* noses. But . . . I am happy to say I exercised great restraint and let them run on ahead of us. Willie was way in front, holding his nose and squawking.

When the boys were out of our hearing range, I tried to talk fast as we walked back to town. "Listen," I said, "we've got to talk about that dead man and about the Widow Watson. I think she knows what we saw. I'm afraid she might be after us, too, and — "

"I got to tell you about the mayor," R. J. interrupted. "Come on, let's walk by his house, and I'll show you — "

"No! R. J., I don't want to walk by his house. Those boys might be there and they'll get me riled up again. Besides, I want you to hush and listen to me. I saw something in Galveston that —"

"Mayor Seamore bought something in Galveston and brought it back with him."

"He always does. Usually a new trinket for his wife."

"Slaves."

59

"What?"

"He bought slaves. I was at the wharf when they unloaded them, the day before you got back. There was three in all. Two field hands and a kitchen maid. And Sadie! *She* was the kitchen maid!"

Leave it to R. J. to steal my thunder.

Papa seemed unusually distracted after supper that night. I was certain he had been told about Willie Barlow's nose, and waiting for him to mention it was like waiting for disaster to strike. I was actually relieved when he finally got around to asking for an explanation for what I'd done.

"I hit Willie Barlow," I said.

"I know that. I'm asking why."

I tried to think of what to say, but words failed me. "He . . . said I wasn't ladylike," I finally managed to stammer.

Papa gave me a funny look and was silent for a long time. "Surely you know you defeated your purpose if you were trying to convince him you *are* a lady," he said at length and very gravely.

"Yes sir," I answered contritely.

I thought I knew what was coming next. I would be instructed to apologize publicly to Willie and to pledge myself to something like washing all the windows in the church to atone for my sin. And I would probably be confined to my room for several days.

But Papa got a far-off look on his face, like he'd forgotten what we were talking about. He stood up and started for the door, leaving me sitting, then he turned around and looked at me as if he had just remembered I was sitting there. "You must learn to control your temper," he said. He started to walk out again, but turned back once more and said, "You must help the sexton sweep the church out Saturday in preparation for Sunday services."

Right then I started to worry about Papa. Helping the sexton sweep out the church wouldn't atone for a little sin like *wishing* I could sock Willie — much less drawing blood. I wasn't inclined to argue with Papa, though. Anyway, I figured I'd saved up some extra atonement by attending Mrs. Seamore's charm and deportment classes as long as I had.

And there was a class to attend that Tuesday. Let me say right off that I tried extra hard that day, but it's very difficult to have social grace when you have dead men and slave auctions on your mind. I made a disaster of the whole day, starting with when we had to read poetry aloud.

Mrs. Seamore says it's a sign of grace and good breeding to be able to read poetry well, but I had forgotten that we were supposed to have a sonnet picked out to read aloud that day, so I had to pick one on the spot. Luckily, Andrea Bowen had brought several books of poetry along with her. I chose *The Works of William Shakespeare,* thinking it would be hard to get off on the wrong foot with a writer Mrs. Seamore is so fond of.

Not having much time to choose, I read the first thing I saw when I opened the book. It started out, "That God forbid that made me first your slave." But I read it wrong, saying, "God forbid that slaves be made."

"You're being fresh, impertinent, and inattentive, Miss McCluster. I insist that you be more respectful and that you pay attention, else I will have to speak with your parents," Mrs. Seamore said. "It is my understanding that you need these classes perhaps more urgently than most after last Sunday's episode. I suggest you conduct yourself properly."

She just went on and on until I was mortified. I *knew* she was talking about me giving Willie a bloody nose and so did everybody else. But I guess misquoting Shakespeare is as much a sin to Mrs. Seamore as swearing is to some, so she felt justified in what she was doing to me.

I was resolved to try harder though, as she instructed me to finish reading the rest of the sonnet. It did seem a waste of time, since I couldn't imagine myself ever being in a situation of needing to read aloud to my company things about being so much in love I felt like a slave. But I went on anyway, fool that I am.

Actually, I did all right until I got to the end of the sonnet. It goes:

> *I am to wait though waiting so be hell,*
> *Not blame your pleasure, be it ill or well.*

Mrs. Seamore just plain had a fit. I don't know what she got so upset about — it was Shakespeare doing all the cussing and saying waiting is hell, not me. Although I am inclined to agree with Shakespeare, especially when it comes to waiting for the end of charm and deportment class.

She said I'd picked that poem out just to show off and to embarrass the class. I got through that disaster just by sitting still and letting her blow off steam while the girls snickered, and while I felt embarrassed.

I was miserable by the time refreshment period rolled around, knowing I would be the outcast of the afternoon. But Lilly Downs came up to me, giving me a sly grin.

"Why, Sarah," she said. "I didn't know you could be

so delightfully wicked! I wish I'd found that sonnet first. Do you know any really good racy parts in Shakespeare? I hear his plays are just full of them."

"No, Lilly, nothing you'd find interesting," I said. "You'd find Shakespeare tame compared to *Passion's Flower*." I had seen her reading a dime novel by that name before school was out. She was hiding it behind her history book.

"Oh have you read that too?" she asked. "What did you think about the part where it says George takes Elizabeth in his arms while they're all alone by the crashing sea, and then he —"

"I haven't read it Lilly," I interrupted.

"Oh, come on now Sarah, you can't fool me."

I guess I would have had to argue with her if Amanda Spencer hadn't come up to me and asked me point-blank if I had really bloodied Willie's nose.

"Sure I did," I said, feeling out of sorts because of the way things were going, "and I'll do it again if he makes me mad enough."

Amanda backed away, wide-eyed and careful, like she was afraid of me. I didn't have time to explain to her that she needn't worry, that *her* nose was in no danger, before Mrs. Seamore called us back to the parlor to practice the embroidery cross-stitch.

It's such an easy stitch I have a hard time keeping my mind on what I'm doing. That's what caused me to stick my finger, I suppose. But the strange thing is, I was so preoccupied I didn't know I'd stuck my finger until I saw the little drops of blood all over the pillow slip I was embroidering. There were also two or three spots on my apron.

Mrs. Seamore saw the spots at about the same time I did. She rolled her eyes, like she couldn't believe there was another creature on earth as dumb and awkward as Sarah McCluster.

"Go to the cistern pump in the back and get some cold water on those spots before the blood sets," she said in a voice that sounded weary.

I hurried out to the back and pumped as hard as I could, listening for the gurgle that meant the water had reached the top. I was holding my apron under the water, when I sensed someone looking at my back. I turned and there she was, dressed in a brown muslin dress that hung loosely on her slender body. We stared at each other for awhile before I got my wits about me enough to speak.

"Hello," I said.

She didn't reply but continued to stare at me.

"Sissy! Sissy! Where you at?" Bella called from inside the building that served as a kitchen. I recognized Bella's voice. She walked out of the kitchen and took the girl's arm. "What you a-doin' out here? You botherin' one of Miz Seamore's charm and deportment girls? She'll hang your hide on the door post if you do. Now get back in there and peel turnips."

The girl just looked at her blankly, until Bella turned her around and pointed to the kitchen, then gave her a gentle swat on her behind. The girl hurried away. "I swan it's hard to make her understand, her not knowin' any English talk," Bella said wiping her hands on her apron. "What you a-doin' out here anyway, Miss Sarah?" she asked.

"I stuck my finger and got blood on my apron. Had to wash it off."

Bella squinted at my apron. "You done a good job. It ain't stained, but it will have to be fresh starched. You go on back in the house now," she said as she started back for her kitchen.

"Bella, wait!" I called.

"What is it, child?" Bella asked, turning back to look at me. Her voice sounded a little weary, too, but in a different way than Mrs. Seamore's did.

"She's new. That girl I mean."

"Yes'm she's new. And I got to train her. Lord knows I need help, but she ain't goin' to be much help till she's proper trained."

"But she'll be company for you, Bella."

"Don't know 'bout that. Little thing cries all time. Misses her mammy, I reckon. But she'll get over it. Jes' like I done."

"Where . . . Where did she come from?"

Bella gave me a funny look. "Galveston, I reckon," she said and turned back once again toward the kitchen.

"Bella — ?"

"Don't ask me no more. That's all I know."

I could tell by the way Bella was acting she knew the girl was new stock, fresh from Africa and brought over illegally by some slave runner.

"I was just going to ask her name. What did you call her? Sissy, wasn't it?"

Bella turned back to me. "Sissy, yes'm. That's her name."

"Did she tell you that?"

"Best I could make out, that's what she said. Somethin' like Sissy Weed. Weed's her last name, I reckon."

"Where's the baby?"

"What baby?"

"The one that was . . . I mean, didn't she . . . ?"

"Sissy's got no baby. Why, she's just a baby herself. What you talkin' 'bout, Miss Sarah?"

"Oh, I . . . I guess I was just wondering if maybe she had a baby sister or brother or something." I had to be careful, letting things slip like that. After all, I wasn't

66

supposed to have ever seen Sissy Weed before. "I best get back to my cross-stitching," I said, hurrying away.

It didn't do me much good to get back to class, since I had a harder-than-ever time concentrating. Mrs. Seamore said my cross-stitches looked like a rail fence after a cyclone. Lilly thought that was terribly funny. She snorted like a pig trying to keep from giggling out loud, and Mrs. Seamore sent her from the room.

Mama had given me strict instructions to come straight home after class. For fear, I suppose, that I would bloody another nose if I dallied anywhere. I hoped I'd see R. J. as I walked home so I could tell him that I'd seen the girl and that she had a name. But I didn't see a soul except one old camel off in the distance. Hi Jolly was sure taking his time about getting them rounded up for the army, it seemed.

As I passed by the church, which is right next to our house, it occurred to me that Papa was probably in there working on his sermon. He was always telling the congregation that he welcomes anyone with problems and troubles to come by and talk to him. I wondered if that went for his daughter too. Sissy Weed, the other slaves and the dead man were weighing mighty heavy on my mind. I decided I'd stop in to see him.

I had stopped in to talk to Papa at other times before, of course. Never with such a big problem maybe, but often enough that I knew his habits. I could tell, for example, by the way his pen scratched the paper, whether his sermon would be a boring one or a real humdinger.

If it was to be a blistering one, he'd be scratching that pen and flying over the paper. He'd splatter ink all over the place stabbing his pen into the inkwell, like the devil's spear into the soul of the damned. It would be hard to get his attention long enough to talk to him. When I looked inside his study this time, I saw his tall slender body with his back to me, seated at his desk. He was just sitting there, staring into space. He would scribble a few words every now and then and scratch them out right after he wrote them. That meant it was probably going to be one of his dull sermons.

"Hello Sarah," Papa said as soon as he saw me. He seemed really glad to see me. Probably because it gave him an excuse not to write his sermon. "What have you been up to lately?" he asked, laying his pen aside.

"I've been to charm and deportment."

"Oh yes, of course, and what did you do today in class?"

He was really not in the mood for his sermon, if he was willing to listen to an answer to that.

"We read some poetry, and I learned to embroider the cross-stitch," I said.

"Good. Good." He nodded his head and tried to look interested.

"I stuck my finger and got blood on my new apron."

"Oh?"

"Wasn't too bad. Mrs. Seamore sent me out to the cistern pump to wash the blood off with cold water. Bella said the stain didn't set, but my apron will need starching."

"Your mother will be glad to hear that neither your finger nor your apron are past saving."

I smiled at his little joke and said, "Bella's got a new kitchen girl to help her."

Papa got a funny look on his face, but he didn't say anything. I plunged ahead. "She can't talk English. Bella said she speaks a heathen tongue. What language do you suppose it is?"

"Couldn't say," Papa said. He picked up his pen and put it to the paper in front of him as if he were going to start writing again.

"Do you suppose it could be African?"

Papa put down his pen and looked at the wall in front of his desk before he turned slowly to look at me again. "Now what makes you ask that?" he said.

"Well, black people come from Africa, and . . ."

"She couldn't be fresh from Africa, Sarah. It's illegal to bring new slaves into this country."

"But just because it's illegal doesn't mean some people don't —"

"Run along, Sarah, I've got work to do."

"But Papa, I just wanted —"

"I said I have work to do!"

Papa seldom speaks to me in such a harsh manner, and I was startled and hurt that he had done so now. I turned quickly and left the church.

Papa didn't have to tell me it was illegal to bring new slaves into the country; I already knew that. What I wanted to know was what to do about it once they were here. I just couldn't keep the image out of my mind of Sissy and her frightened eyes. And I could still see the baby who had clung to her. That had to be her brother or sister. Where was that baby now? And where was their mother?

I just had to talk to somebody about it, and there was nobody but R. J. to talk to now. So upset was I, that I decided to go see him, even against my mother's orders. I found him in his front yard chucking rocks at a camel that had been nibbling at radish tops in the La Salle's vegetable patch.

The camel ignored the rocks for awhile, but when one hit him on the forelock, he turned and hissed, sending a spray of camel spit right at us. That sent us both racing for the back of the house.

"Damn that beast!" R. J. said, his voice quivering from fright.

I wasn't used to hearing swear words, unless it was

Shakespeare, but I wasn't up to calling R. J. down for it just then.

"Why'd they set them critters loose on us anyway?" R. J. asked. I could tell he was embarrassed by his fear. "It's a downright shame, and a mortal danger."

"Mortal danger?"

"It is. Camel spit is poison. Miss Cassie says it will raise boils and sores and make you bilious unto death. Why'd they set 'em free to torment us?"

"You know how Miss Cassie exaggerates. Willie Barlow didn't get bilious. and he didn't die when he got spit on. And you also know why the beasts were set free. 'Cause the widow wouldn't pay for 'em. She had her contraband to worry about."

R. J. turned to look at me, forgetting about camel spit for the moment. "Did you see her yet?" he asked.

I knew he wasn't talking about the widow. He was talking about Sissy.

"Yes. Bella says her name sounds like Sissy Weed."

"Sissy Weed," he said, trying it. "She looks pitiful don't she?"

"There ought to be some way we could help her."

"How?"

"I don't know, but there ought to be a way. If we could just tell somebody she's not really supposed to be a slave. That she got here illegally. Maybe then they'd send her and her family back home to Africa."

"We'd have to prove it," R. J. said. "That she was brought over illegally. And I reckon that won't be easy."

"Why would we have to do that?" I asked. "Why couldn't we just tell the sheriff and let him do the proving?"

R. J.'s dark eyes seemed to pity my ignorance. "Tell the sheriff the *mayor* bought an illegal slave? Now where would that get us?"

"Well, we ought to try something."

70

"You're right. But let's ease into it. We could start by asking questions about legality and things like that."

"Asking who?"

"How about ole man Lassiter?"

He meant Travis Lassiter the newspaper editor. I told him it was worth a try, so we walked to the newspaper building on Alameda Street.

For all the good ideas he gets, R. J. never seems to know how to carry them out. That was obvious as soon as we walked in the front door of the *Weekly Sentinel,* and saw Mr. Lassiter chewing on a cigar and hunched over a tray full of metal type. Mr. Lassiter asked what he could do for us, and R. J. just stood there staring at him. It was up to me to bail us out.

I told him we were interested in the slavery question because we were beginning to discuss current issues in charm and deportment class. I told him I needed some information from some of his papers in order to prepare myself for the discussion. That wasn't the truth of course. We never discuss anything more weighty than a recipe for pound cake, but as I've said, lying comes easy to me.

He turned all of the copies of his past newspapers over to us, but it turned out we never found exactly what we were looking for in any of them. Instead, he told us something that stopped our search.

"Country's in a stew 'bout the slavery question, that's for sure," he said, puffing his cigar. "Been brewing for years."

"Yes, sir," we both said.

"Abolitionists, they're called. Them that wants to abolish the institution. Can't make up my mind how I feel about the issue. If we set 'em all free, what will they do with themselves? Don't know how to take care of themselves. They'll all die. Besides it will ruin the economy of the South for sure without their labor in the fields. On the other hand, maybe it ain't right to own another human being. Some kind of compromise is probably best, like the law of 1820, that says keep the old slaves and their offspring, but makes it illegal to bring in new slaves."

"Really? The law of 1820, you say? Did you have a story about it?" I asked. I felt a surge of excitement, because now it seemed we were getting somewhere.

"Nope. Didn't have a newspaper here then. Didn't have a town even. Fact is, Texas wasn't even a state then. It still belonged to Mexico. So whatever the U.S. Congress did didn't effect folks here."

"Well, did the law stop folk from bringing in slaves?" I asked. Of course I knew the answer to my question, but I had to keep him talking.

"Of course not," he said. "Laws don't stop anything there's money in. Just slows it down a little. Slave traders smuggle them in."

"Really? What happens if the smugglers get caught?" R. J. asked.

"Not easy to catch," Mr. Lassiter said, biting down on his cigar and squinting at the smoke. "Somebody'd have to inform on them. Not many in the South would do that. Some from fear of the slave traders, and some for wanting to have an abundance of slaves in the country to keep the price down."

"Did you ever hear of anybody who got caught?" I asked.

"Oh, I reckon there's been a few. Some states have tried to make it profitable for informers. Take here in the state of Texas. If the trader is caught, the state sells his new slaves and gives the proceeds to the informer as a reward."

"You mean the new stock is sold as slaves anyway,

even though they've been brought here illegally?" I asked.

"That's the law in most of the South," Mr. Lassiter said, "and when they've been sold once, they're legal slaves from them on. And of course, it's not difficult for a slave trader to provide an auctioneer with a false bill of sale to prove they were legal to begin with."

I felt as down and out as R. J. looked. We both knew now that it wouldn't do much good to try to prove Sissy Weed was brought over illegally. She was doomed to slavery.

"Well, thanks, Mr. Lassiter," I said. "I won't take up your time any longer."

"But what about your discussion you were preparing for?" he asked, stopping me before I reached the door.

"Oh, that. You've told me so much, I'll have to sort it all out in my mind for awhile before I look for anything else."

"Don't just skim the surface of this issue. There's more," he said a little crossly, like maybe he wished we'd help him sort out the questions in his mind for him. "Some good anecdotes might liven your discussion up a little, and you'll find plenty of those in the *Weekly Sentinel*. Like the one last year over in Brazoria County. A band of Negroes planned an escape to Mexico where slavery has been abolished. But they were caught and hanged, along with the white men who tried to help them. You ought to look that up. It was in the paper. Just about a year ago, I think."

"We'll be back sometime and look that story up, but we got to be going now," R. J. said. He gave me a wide-eyed look that told me there were some things that scared him more than camel spit and biliousness.

"We can't help her," he said when we were outside

73

the newspaper office. "She's a legal slave now, and if we try to help her escape we'll be hanged."

He was right, and I knew it. There was nothing I could say.

I don't know what got into me, but I thought I just had to see Sissy Weed again, so I made up an excuse to go by the Seamores' house. Mrs. Seamore seemed surprised when I showed up in her parlor. Of course she was careful to tell me it was a "pleasant surprise."

"Please sit down," she said. "I'll call for tea."

"Oh, no thank you Ma'am. I can't stay for tea. You see, I have lost my thimble. Would you mind if I took a look around the cistern pump to see if I dropped it there?"

I'd committed the sin of lying again. My thimble was at home in my sewing box. As I said, I don't know what got into me.

"Well of course, my dear," Mrs. Seamore said. "And I will help you look."

"Drat the luck!" I said under my breath, that being as close as I was willing to come to swearing just then. My sins were mounting high as the hump on a camel's back as it was.

"What was that you said, my dear?" Mrs. Seamore asked.

"Oh, I just said, 'I can look.' What I mean is, there's no need for you to trouble yourself."

"Now, aren't you thoughtful," Mrs. Seamore said, taking my hand and leading me to the back part of the house. "Where were you standing? Right about here?" she asked, when we got out to the pump.

"I think so."

"Are you sure you brought your thimble out here with you?" She was looking down at the wet ground around the pump.

"Yes, Ma'am," I said, trying to look as if I was searching the ground, too. Actually, I was looking toward the kitchen house, hoping to catch a glimpse of Sissy. I could hear sounds coming from there, so I knew someone was inside.

"You didn't drop it down in the cistern, did you?"

"Oh no . . . I would have heard the splash."

"Yes, of course."

We searched the ground for several more minutes, and Mrs. Seamore kept straightening her back and saying, "Oh, mercy." Finally she asked if I would like another thimble as a gift.

"That's very kind of you, Ma'am, but my own thimble has special meaning to me. Mama gave it to me, don't you know."

"Yes, of course," Mrs. Seamore said again, sounding a little annoyed this time. "But I'm sure she'd understand," she added. "These things do happen."

"I'll just keep looking," I said.

"A nice new silver one? I saw some in Galveston."

I smiled and shook my head. Mrs. Seamore looked more annoyed than ever, but I knew my persistance was about to pay off. "If you don't mind, I'll look around just a little longer, but let me help you back to the parlor and into a chair so you can rest your back. I'll ask Bella to bring you some tea," I said with as much charm as I could muster.

"Such a thoughtful child," she said, letting me lead her back to the house. "You won't exhaust yourself with the search will you?"

"Oh, no Ma'am."

"Very well," she said, as she settled herself into a chair in the parlor. "And do send Bella."

"Yes, Ma'am," I said, hurrying to the back again as quickly as I could. Bella was stepping out of the kitchen house just as I reached the back door.

"Miss Sarah, what you doin' here?" she asked.

I told her my story about the lost thimble and mentioned that Mrs. Seamore had exhausted herself helping me look. "She wants you to bring her tea now," I said.

Bella turned to the kitchen grumbling a little, but she soon came back carrying a teapot and cup along with cream and sugar on a tray. As soon as she was out of sight, I headed for the kitchen. Peeking inside the open door, I saw Sissy standing at the stove stirring a steaming pot of something that smelled like fish chowder. The heat from the tiny one-room building felt like standing in front of an oven with the door open. Sissy looked very hot, tired, and uncomfortable. She seemed to sense my eyes on her, and she turned to look. Her own eyes grew wider when she saw me.

"Hello, Sissy," I said.

She just stared at me and didn't say a word.

"My name is Sarah. Sarah," I said, pointing to myself.

She gave me a quizzical look, then put down her spoon and pointed to herself. "Si Si Wee," she said. She was telling me her name, using rhythmical dancing sounds that were strange to my ears. They were sounds I knew I couldn't duplicate. The best I could do was to call her what Bella had called her.

"Sissy Weed," I said.

My attempt seemed to disappoint her, judging by the look on her face.

"I saw you get off the ship," I said.

Sissy's eyes grew wide again, and she repeated the word: "Ship."

"Where's the baby?" I asked.

She gave me another puzzled look, so I cradled my arms and rocked them as if I were holding a baby. Tears filled her eyes, and I knew she had understood my question.

"Maybe he's with your Mama," I said, hoping I could make her feel better.

"Mama," she repeated, and said something in her own language. Then when she said, "Mama slave," I knew Bella must have taught her a few words.

To my surprise, Sissy took my hand and led me away from the kitchen to the side of the house that faced the bay. "Fetch Mama," Sissy said, pointing to the water.

"Oh dear," I said, feeling uncomfortable. "I'm afraid that wouldn't be easy. Your mama's been sold into slavery, and so have you."

Her face was another question. "Please, thank you?" she asked, using more words I knew Bella had taught her.

"Sissy Weed slave," I said pointing to her and speaking slowly. "Mama slave. No find . . . er . . . no fetch," I said shaking my head. I'm not sure that Sissy understood the words, but she seemed to grasp the meaning because I saw tears fill her eyes again. This time they spilled over the rims and down her high-boned cheeks.

"Si Si Wee slave no," she said shaking her head. She said something else in her own language, and this time I was the one who missed the words but got the meaning. I think she was explaining to me who she was. Whatever it was, I know she did not think of herself as a slave.

"Sissy! Sissy, where is you?" We both heard Bella

call. She stepped into the kitchen and placed her hands on her hips, showing her displeasure with me. "Now what are you doing in here, Miss Sarah?"

"I was . . . I was just talking to Sissy . . ."

"Well now you run along and look for your thimble. Sissy's got work to do. I got to show her how to kill chickens and dress 'em for supper tonight."

"Kill?" Sissy Weed asked. She said the word as if she had heard it before.

"Yes, chile. We got to kill 'em to eat 'em," Bella said. "You run along now," she said, turning back to me. "Go look for that thimble somewhere else."

"I'm going," I said, not wanting to get Sissy into trouble. I ran around to the front of the house, and there I saw Mrs. Seamore sitting on her veranda sipping tea.

"Sarah," she called as I tried to slip by, "did you find your thimble?"

"Oh, yes," I said, hurrying away. "My thimble is safe."

L ater, when I told R. J. about my conversation with Sissy, it seemed to upset him as much as it had me. But he couldn't come up with any ideas for helping her. I must say I was disappointed that his imagination had failed him at such a critical time.

I was worried about Sissy. If we couldn't think of a way to help her, at least I would like to be able to comfort her. Charm and deportment class was cancelled the next week, though, and for the first time ever I was disappointed. I would not see Sissy Weed. A notice in the *Weekly Sentinel* told why the class was cancelled:

This week, His Honor the Mayor and Mrs. Alexander Seamore will have as their guests, Mrs. Ashworth Bottoms of Beaumont and New Orleans, as well as Captain John Reed of the merchant ship *Glory Star,* which is back in port. The lady being a friend of Mrs. Seamore's from their school days in New Orleans, and the captain being a friend and business associate of His Honor the Mayor. Both will be honored during an evening of chamber music and other gaieties to which select citizens of Indianola have been invited.

The captain would be at the party! The thought of it

frightened me. I knew we girls from charm and deportment would be among the "select citizens" invited. Mrs. Seamore couldn't throw a party without us.

Sure enough, Mrs. Seamore sent a note on her jasmine scented paper asking me and Mama and Papa to come. She also asked me to prepare a piece to play on the piano in honor of Mrs. Ashworth Bottoms of Beaumont and New Orleans.

Neither R. J. nor his mother would be at the party. Mrs. Seamore does not consider the La Salles "select," except when she's short of dancing partners for us girls at our soirees and she has to call on R. J.

When the evening of chamber music and other gaieties rolled around, Mama and Papa seemed less anxious to go than I, which is a switch. But they pretended to be "charmed," just as Mama said they were in the response she sent to Mrs. Seamore. And they both kept saying how glad they were that I was taking an interest in cultural events. All I could think of was that it would be another chance for me to see how Sissy Weed was doing, even if I did dread seeing the captain.

When we arrived at the party, Sissy was nowhere in sight. One of the garden boys they were trying to train as a butler, met us at the door. I saw Bella, too. She brought a tray of delicacies to the parlor, set them on a table and disappeared. I saw the captain drinking a glass of wine with His Honor. The Widow Watson stood nearby.

When we were being introduced to the captain, I held my breath the whole time for fear he had seen me hiding in the brush down by the cove, and would recognize me. He didn't seem to, though. I let all my air out in a noisy sigh that made Mama turn pink with embarrassment.

Mama and Papa and I were presented to Mrs. Ashworth Bottoms of Beaumont and New Orleans. "Mc-

Cluster?" She asked, looking through her hand-held spectacles, first at me and then at Mama and Papa. "Of the Virginia McClusters?"

"The Arkansas McClusters," Papa said.

Her nose twitched a little as if she had just smelled something unpleasant. "Oh, I see," she said. Then she put her twitching nose up in the air and walked away.

Just then Mrs. Seamore clapped her hands and said we would begin the chamber music, and that she was pleased to present the first selection. Which, she said, she had composed herself especially for the honored guests.

After that everybody just had to sit there listening to Mrs. Seamore play the piano and sing something she called "Hark, Hark, The Lark Doth Blithely Call." It had lots of trills and runs in it and lots of high notes which Mrs. Seamore did her best to sing. Mama tapped me on the knee twice to get me to pay attention, because I kept looking over my shoulder to see if Sissy Weed had entered the room.

I was truly thankful when "Hark, Hark, The Lark Doth Blithely Call" was over, and I think the honored guests were, too. Every time I squirmed around to look for Sissy Weed, I saw the honored guests. Mrs. Ashworth Bottoms had that look again, like she smelled something bad, and the captain was on his third glass of wine.

Lilly Downs was next. She played Beethoven's *Fur Elise*. When she finished, Mrs. Seamore stood up and announced that Miss Sarah McCluster would now entertain us with a selection of her choosing.

My heart came to my mouth. I had been so preoccupied with other things, namely Sissy Weed, and the dead man, that I clean forgot to prepare. The only thing I could think of to do was to plead that I was physically unable. Signaling for Mrs. Seamore to step aside, I whispered to her that my poor finger, the one I had stuck with the embroidery needle, was giving me trouble.

"Why Sarah McCluster, I never heard of such a thing," she said. "It was no more than a scratch. You've got stage fright!"

"Oh no, Ma'am, it's not that at all," I protested, but she wouldn't listen.

"Stage fright of course," she said, "and that's what these little gatherings are for — to help you learn to overcome fear of performing for an audience. Come along now and learn to be at ease displaying talent and good graces."

That woman wouldn't have let me off if I had come to the evening of gaiety with my hand chopped off to a bloody stump.

The only thing I could think of to play was, *In the Sweet Bye and Bye.* I know that's not what Mrs. Seamore calls chamber music. It was plain old church music, but I had got Papa out of a pinch once at a funeral with that piece when our organist got sick on fresh turnips. Mama and Papa both looked proud and smiled big when I finished, but Mrs. Seamore looked awful put out. Luckily, some of the other girls had some nice pieces by Chopin and Bach prepared. That cheered her up some.

In fact, she seemed in a right good mood by the time Bella came out with some punch and some little cakes, and we broke up for refreshments. It was beginning to look like I wasn't going to see anything of Sissy Weed. I had just decided there was nothing else to do but have some of the cake and punch and hope the evening would end soon, when I saw her. She was bringing out a pitcher full of lemonade to add to the punch bowl.

I smiled at her, and she gave me a tiny timid smile in return. Then I saw her eyes meet the captain's. She stopped dead still for a split second, and her hands began to tremble. She let out a frightened cry and dropped the pitcher of lemonade, letting it splatter all over the voluminous skirts of Mrs. Ashworth Bottoms of Beaumont and New Orleans.

The lady screamed of course, and everyone rushed to her, trying to wipe off her skirt and hush her cries. Mrs. Seamore was obviously embarrassed. She rushed at Sissy Weed.

"Get that wretched urchin out of here," she said, shoving Sissy ruthlessly toward Bella.

Sissy Weed began to cry and to chatter in the unknown tongue. I understood only one word, "kill." She pointed to the captain as she said it and the whole room grew quiet except for Mrs. Ashworth Bottom's cries.

"Kill," she said again, almost in a whisper.

What did she mean, I wondered. Was it just a word she had learned from Bella? Or did she mean she wanted to kill the captain?

"What is that girl saying?" one of the gentlemen at the party asked. She must be speaking in that heathen African tongue."

"I know the language," Captain Reed said. "I've sailed the Gold Coast of Africa."

"Then what is it she's babbling?" His Honor asked. It didn't seem to bother him that it had become obvious he had bought illegal "new stock."

"The darkie is accusing me of killing a man," the captain said.

You could have heard a pin drop. Even Mrs. Bottoms stopped her crying. Then the mayor broke the silence with a guffaw. "Preposterous!" he said. "Where would she get such a notion?"

"Superstition?" the captain proposed. "Perhaps she thinks I look like an evil spirit."

His remark brought laughter from the crowd and the captain smiled as he took another sip from his wine glass.

Sissy Weed clung to Bella's shirts and her frightened eyes never left the captain.

"Take her away!" Mrs. Seamore commanded Bella. "I'll see she's dealt with tomorrow." She turned to Mrs. Ashworth Bottoms. "I'm so sorry," she said, "but you know it takes time and liberal doses of the switch to get them into shape."

I don't know what Mrs. Ashworth Bottoms replied. My eyes and my attention were on the Widow Watson. She was staring at me with a look that sent chills through my soul. Did she know that I knew what Sissy Weed meant?

The next day I knew what I had to do. I remembered that Hi Jolly had said he could understand the language of the black Africans. I hoped that meant he knew more than just the word for "a certain part of a monkey's body," and that I could get him to interpret Sissy Weed's story for the sheriff. Then maybe the sheriff would believe what R. J. and I had been trying to tell him about the dead man on Powderhorn Bayou.

I told R. J. my plan, and he went with me to look for Hi Jolly. We figured we'd find him wherever the camels were.

I knew the army was due in sometime that week to help Hi Jolly and Mendez drive the beasts to Camp Verde on the western plains where the rest of the army's ships of the desert are kept. That meant Hi Jolly and Mendez should be almost finished rounding them up.

Since it looked like it would be my last chance to ride a camel, I thought I'd kill two birds with one stone — get Hi Jolly to interpret Sissy's words for the sheriff, *and* ride a camel.

We saw one old camel way off up the bayou, but there was no Hi Jolly. We waited around for him a little while, but it was just too hot to wait very long. We decided it was probably too hot for Hi Jolly and Mendez to be working, too.

It was one of those days when the clouds roll in off the gulf, holding in the heat and making the air feel thick and sticky as wild grape jelly. That's the kind of weather that puts me in a bad humor. Being out by the bayou with all the gnats and mosquitoes nipping at me made it even worse. I told R. J. I was going back to town, and I would have, if we hadn't run into Willie Barlow on the way back.

"Who you spyin' on this time?" he asked when he saw me.

"Don't start in on me again, Willie. Just hush your mouth, or I'll hush it for you."

"You ain't got the nerve to do it again."

R. J. stepped between us. "Leave her alone, Willie Barlow," he said.

"Let me at him!" I said.

"I was only jokin'," Willie said, losing his bravado and covering his nose with his hand. "I knew you weren't spyin' really. I knew you were just out there lookin' for her."

"Looking for who? What do you mean?" I asked.

"Why the Seamores' new girl," Willie said. "Didn't you know she got a whippin' for that mess she made at the Seamore's house? And now she's run away. His Honor has rode out to the edge of town to meet the army. He's going to ask 'em to look all up and down the beaches for the new slave girl before they get to rounding up the camels. He's already sent instructions to have the storehouses around the wharves searched."

"Oh Lordy Mercy," I said, looking at R. J. His face had gone white as sunbleached linen and his eyes looked like saucers. I knew he was thinking the same thing I was. If Sissy Weed was caught, her fate would be the same as the runaway slaves Brazoria County — the ones that Mr. Lassiter at the newspaper had told us about. She could be hanged.

"They're gonna comb the beaches and all those buildings along the wharves," Willie said again.

"Come along, R. J.," I said impatiently, "We can leave the search to His Honor Mayor Seamore. Let's go look for the camels."

"But, I thought you just said it was too hot to — "

"Come on, R. J.," I said, urging him on. "The camels, remember?"

Finally R. J. caught on that I just wanted to get away from Willie so we could talk. We struck out for the bayou, leaving Willie on the edge of town, holding his nose protectively.

We hadn't gone far when we ran into Hi Jolly and Mendez. They had rope halters around the necks of two camels and were headed toward the old army corrals with them.

"Drat the luck!" I said to no one in particular. "They're going to have the beasts all corraled for the army before I get my ride."

"Hah!" said Mendez, who had overheard me. "It will be a cold day in hell before we get these animals corraled if we don't get help from the army. And now we hear the mayor has got other plans for the soldiers. It's just the Arab and me."

"I am the best cimmel man in the world," Hi Jolly said, "and I have just turned my friend into the second best cimmel man in the world, but what can we do when the army goes back on its promise to help?" He put his arm around Mendez's shoulder as he spoke. Their quarrel was apparently forgotten now that they were both mad at the army. "I am afraid they may expect us to drive the beasts to the desert by ourselves. But they are Bedouin thieves if they think I'll do it without more pay."

"It would take too long without the army's help," Mendez agreed. "Even for the best and the second best camel man in the world. What could be so important to the mayor and to the army that they are saying now they don't have time to help?"

"You mean you don't know?" R. J. asked.

They gave each other a blank look and shook their heads.

"It's the slave girl. The mayor's new girl. She's run away. The mayor has asked the army to help them look for her," I said.

"One poor black African child against the army on horses?" Hi Jolly asked. "Even a Bedouin would not stoop so low."

"Hi Jolly," I said in a shaky voice. "She is African. You speak her language, don't you?"

"Hadji Ali speaks some of the African tongues, yes. Why do you ask?"

"I need . . . We need you to interpret . . . She knows something important about the dead man on Powderhorn Bayou. Mendez knows the man I'm talking about. The little black girl knows something the sheriff should know, but you must interpret for her. If . . . if they find her."

"Are you saying, Senorita, that the slave girl may know who killed the man?" Mendez asked.

I nodded my head.

"May the Holy Mother watch over and protect her," Mendez said, crossing himself. "If the killer is a white man, then we must pray that she never tells her story. They will say she is lying and beat her for it."

"May the armies of Allah fight for her," Hi Jolly said.

"But *we* must try to help her. They can't say she's lying. Please say you'll help," I pleaded.

"I will help if I can," Hi Jolly said. "I am no infidel who sacrifices children. But it is better that she be asleep in the arms of the Prophet than rescued by the army."

"May all the Saints protect her," Mendez said. The two of them moved away from us, arm and arm, each trying to top the blessing of the other for poor Sissy Weed.

"Where do you suppose she is?" R. J. asked as they moved away.

"There's no telling," I said. "She doesn't know her way around this town or the beaches at all. But we've got to find her before anyone else does."

"If I was going to hide, I'd go to one of those empty sheds on the wharves," R. J. said as we began walking back toward town.

"Willie said that's one of the first places they'll look."

"It's awful hot," R. J. said. "Maybe they won't start looking till it gets a little later and cools off some. Maybe that'll give us a chance to find her first."

By the time we got to his house, he had a plan worked out for how we could systematically search the wharves. "I'll get a jug of water and some cold biscuits to keep us going," he said, walking in his front door. "We'll keep looking till night if we have to."

I followed R. J. into his house and into the kitchen. He was just reaching for a pan of leftover biscuits that were on top of the oven when Mrs. La Salle came in the back door.

"Well there you are, R. J.," she said. "I've been looking for you all morning. You're to clean out the chicken house for me, remember? It's time you got to work."

"But Mama . . ."

"The shovel and rake are in the toolshed, and there's

fresh straw for the nests in the back." She had R. J. by the arm leading him toward the back door. There wasn't a thing in the world R. J. or I either one could do about it. If we just hadn't come back in the house for those biscuits he wouldn't have gotten snagged. But if it isn't R. J.'s imagination that'll get the best of him one of these days, it'll be his appetite.

I turned and headed for the street again, resolved to start the search for Sissy Weed by myself and to start immediately, even though the weather was getting hotter and stickier by the minute. My first stop was the wharves. There were a few sailors around, and I knew Sissy wouldn't be where anybody could see her.

Maybe she'd be in one of the buildings. I stuck my head in to find out. It had been used to store hay for the army's horses before they moved their unit out to Camp Verde. It was awfully dark and spooky looking, so I stepped in cautiously. Two glowing eyes stared at me from out of the darkness, and for a moment I was too frightened to move. But it was only a rat foraging in the remnants of the army's hay. He ran away from me, apparently more frightened than I was, and disappeared through a hole in the floor. The rat and I had been the only living beings in the building, though. Sissy was nowhere in sight.

I left that building and peered inside several more, but still I found no Sissy Weed. I was becoming more and more discouraged and frightened for her, and the weather continued to add to my dark mood as clouds kept coming in from the gulf like more gray rats running from something. There was going to be a storm for sure, and I had to find Sissy before it hit.

I had wasted my time by taking R. J.'s suggestion to look in the buildings along the wharves, and if I just had not let him do my thinking for me, I would have realized to begin with that it would be a waste of time. Sissy wouldn't hide in the empty buildings along the waterfront because she didn't even know about them. There were only two places, other than the auction block in Galveston, that she knew about. One was the mayor's house, and the other was the cove where she had first come ashore.

The cove! I should have thought of that first. Glancing up at the sky, I knew it was going to rain soon, and from the looks of it, a real downpour. I wouldn't have much time to get out to the cove and back to the house before it started. I headed for Smugglers' Cove, running as fast as I could.

My dress and petticoats kept working up above my knees as I ran. Mrs. Seamore would have been shocked out of her garters, not to mention my mother, but I didn't have time to worry about that. All I could think of was how I wished R. J. had been free to go with me. It would have saved time for him to search one end of the cove while I searched the other.

It had already started to rain by the time I reached the cove, and the sea was dark and boiling. I walked up and down the beach, calling her name, but I could hardly hear my own voice above the sound of the wind and the angry sea.

Finally, as I topped a small rise in the mostly flat beach, I saw her, huddled in a ball as if she were trying to make herself disappear. I came upon her so quickly I almost stepped on her, and we stared at each other a few seconds, both too startled to speak.

The wind drove the rain into my face and wrapped my dress around my knees. My hair had long since come unbraided, and I kept having to brush the wet strands from my eyes.

"We've got to get out of the storm," I said, pointing to

the swells on the water. "It might even be a hurricane. We have to get away from the beach." The wind robbed my words as soon as I uttered them, but I reached my hand toward her, and she seemed to understand. She placed her hand in mind and let me pull her to her feet.

As soon as she stood, I saw her eyes grow even wider and more frightened, and I turned to see several riders on horseback in the distance. They moved toward us in the hard-driving rain, looking like apparitions swimming through liquid air. Quickly, I pushed Sissy Weed to the ground behind the small rise. I had recognized uniforms of the U.S. Army. They were riding along the beach, just as Willie Barlow had said they would. They reined their horses in and stayed in a group for a few seconds, then they broke away, riding in different directions. One of them rode straight for us.

I covered Sissy's frail body with my own, as if I was trying to make her disappear by pushing her into the sand. The howl of the wind and rain was too loud for me to hear the approaching hoofbeats, but I could feel them through the ground beneath me. As the horse came closer, I was certain the rider would be able to hear the sound of my heart pounding.

Suddenly I saw the forelocks of a horse quivering and dancing above me. My skirt pulled loose from where I had it tucked beneath me and flapped in the wind, spooking the horse and causing him to whinny and skitter backwards.

"Allah and the beard of Mohammed!" a voice said.

I looked up into the dark face of Hi Jolly. "In the name of Allah, keep your head down," he snapped. He wheeled his horse and shouted into the wind. "Nobody on this side. Maybe we will stop now and wait for the rains to stop and for the winds to blow no more?"

He rode away, and I waited several minutes longer before I raised my head to look up and down the beach. There were no soldiers in sight. Hi Jolly must have convinced them to wait out the storm before they searched anymore. Praise be to Allah for watching over deceitful Presbyterians.

I t was raining harder, and the sea tried to swallow the shore in a hungry tantrum. I pulled Sissy Weed to her feet, and took her hand as we made our way through the storm. We were both covered with mud, but the rain soon washed it away, leaving us both looking like half drowned kittens.

Before we reached the bayou, I could see that it was running over its banks and even up over the bridge. But I could see someone near the bridge! It was someone in a long black skirt. It was a woman, and she was sawing away at the rope that held the bridge.

"What are you doing? Stop! Stop!" I called. But the woman couldn't hear my words over the roar of the storm. I didn't know whether she saw me or Sissy Weed or not, but I had seen her clearly enough to recognize her. It was the Widow Watson, and whether she had seen us or not, she knew we were out there. Why else would she be destroying the bridge?

Finally she accomplished her task, and I saw the swinging bridge topple into the churning water. The widow turned and ran through the storm back toward town.

It took awhile for Sissy and me to make our way through the wind and rain to the edge of the bayou. We stopped when we reached it, watching the water churning and chewing, and the bridge, dangling and bouncing in the swelling stream. Sissy, still holding tightly to my hand, looked into my face and then at the water. She let go of my hand and stepped into the bayou.

"Sissy!" I called, reaching for her, but she was away from me and in the water up to her knees. I watched her as the water lapped at her thighs, then reached her waist. I screamed as she swayed forward, but she began stroking at the water, swimming the way boys do, but girls are not allowed to try. The water pulled her downstream some, but I saw her grab a bush near the water's edge and pull herself to shore. She stood up, dripping with the muddy bayou water and motioned for me to start across.

"I can't swim!" I cried.

She didn't understand, but kept motioning for me to try.

"I'll drown. I'll die. It's what the widow wanted. Didn't you see her? She cut down the bridge! And I can't swim!"

Sissy at last seemed to understand my fear. She stooped and quickly retrieved a long branch that was floating down the swollen waters and held it out to me, indicating that I was to step into the water and wade until I could reach the branch.

I prayed for courage to do what she was suggesting, but the Lord had no courage to spare. I had to start across with nothing but fear. The swirling water made me dizzy, and I tried frantically to reach for the extended branch before the water was to my chin. I had it in my grasp when my foot struck a rock and I felt myself falling, going down until the water closed around my neck, then covered my mouth, my nose, my eyes. I could see my hair, matted and full of dirt, swirling around my face under water. I tried to scream, but the water filled my mouth. Then I felt two hands under my arms and felt myself being pulled until my head was above the water. Sissy had waded back into the water and, skinny as she was, she was swimming and dragging me to the other side of the bayou.

I was sorely grateful, but I said not a word of thanks, since words were a luxury we could not afford at that moment. We both ran through the storm to town.

In spite of the fact that it was still afternoon, the black sky made it look like dusk, and there was no one on the streets of Indianola. I knew everyone would be inside, but I also knew they would probably be looking out their windows watching the spectacle of the storm. They could see us as well. It was then that I began to wonder why I had been so anxious to get back to town. What was I going to do with Sissy?

It was no plan, but some kind of instinct that led me toward my own home. I could see a light in the window as we drew closer, and I knew Mama would be peering out into the dark storm watching for me. I had to get home before she sent Papa out to look for me, if she hadn't done so already. I prayed that she hadn't. Just to be safe, I addressed my prayer to both Allah and Our Father Which Art In Heaven, being sure now either name was all right, and not wanting to miss any heavenly attention.

The thing to do, I decided, as I pulled Sissy along, was to go around to the back of the house where there were no lights. That way I could get inside without being seen as I approached. But what I was going to do with Sissy, I still did not know.

As we walked toward the back of the house, I saw the church, unlit and looming large in the darkness of the storm. It looked like the house in the parable — the one built on solid rock that doesn't get washed away.

Before we got past the church, I saw the lamplight move to the kitchen, then I saw the back door open just a crack. Mama's voice called my name through the storm. There wasn't time to do much except push open the heavy front door of the church and shove Sissy inside. I couldn't see, before I slammed the door shut, whether she landed on her feet or on her chin. As soon as it was closed, I raced across the backyard, through the kitchen door and into Mama's arms.

Papa was just pulling on his raincoat, preparing to go out to look for me. They were too glad to see me to scold at first, but they got to it soon enough.

"You know better than to be out like that when you see a storm brewing," Mama said, as she tried to unsnarl my hair. "Where were you anyway?"

"Down by the cove," I said.

"What on earth were you doing down by the cove?" Papa asked.

"I heard about the runaway slave. I thought I might see her down there."

"You've got no business chasing after runaway slaves, young lady," he said angrily. "What made you think the runaway would be at the cove, anyway?"

"Well . . . there were soldiers out there searching. I saw them."

"Wandering along the beach alone! Running into soldiers!" Mama threw up her hands in despair.

"What else did you see?" Papa asked, his voice sounding a little strained.

"Well, I saw . . . That is . . . err, uh . . . Oh, I don't know, just —"

"The slave?"

"What?" I was shivering as I sat wrapped in the quilt

Mama had given me, but Papa's questioning was putting me in a sweat.

"Did the army find the slave?" he asked insistently.

"Oh! No. No I don't believe they did."

"Wet as you are, you'd think you'd been swimming in the gulf, instead of just walking on the beach," Mama said as she picked up my things and shook sand and water from them. "Just look at your apron. It looks like it's got that muddy bayou water in it. Ruined! It'll never be white again!"

I was about the apologize for ruining my apron, but I sneezed just then, and it was the sneeze that saved my skin. I got neither a lecture from Mama about ruined aprons nor questions from Papa about runaway slaves. Instead, I was given a hot bath, a dose of cod-liver oil to ward off the grippe, and sent to bed.

As night approached, the storm howled like an angry beast as I lay in bed. Great sheets of rain fell from the sky as it was continually cut open by jagged bolts of lightning. I could sleep not a wink for worrying about Sissy Weed — cold, wet, and alone in the church.

I heard a sudden clattering sound like something being torn apart, and I jumped out of bed and ran to the window at the end of the hall to see what it was. Mama and Papa rushed out of their bedroom too, and joined me at the window. A flash of lightning showed us the backyard filled with tree limbs and fallen leaves. What looked like the roof of someone's house had been thrown into the vegetable patch.

"Look at that!" Mama said. "That looks like boards and shingles from the church roof! Oh the hymnbooks! The new altar cloth the Women's Circle made! Everything will be soaked."

"I'll go see what I can do about bringing them into the house," Papa said. He turned toward the bedroom to get his coat and trousers, and I felt my heart in my mouth. He'd see Sissy Weed if he went to the church.

"You'll do no such thing," Mama said, grabbing Papa's arm and holding it with her tiny delicate hands.

"But what about the hymnbooks and the altar cloths? You said yourself they'll be ruined."

"Better them than you," Mama said emphatically. "Thank God we're safe and dry in the house. You can see to the church in the morning. We'll salvage what we can and the Lord will provide for the rest."

"Do you think it's going to get worse?" I asked. "Is it going to be a full-blown hurricane?"

"Could be," Papa said. He saw the worried look on Mama's face and added quickly, "But the Lord will watch over us."

I got back into my bed wondering if the Lord would watch over Sissy Weed, too. *Probably not*, I thought, hearing the wind scream as it tossed something against the side of the house. He was probably going to leave it up to me. And if He was, I'd better get busy.

I got out of bed and pulled my cloak out of my wardrobe chest. Throwing it across my shoulders, I tiptoed down the hall to the stairs. Just as I reached the top of the landing, I heard a stirring and thought I had awakened Papa. I stopped to listen, hoping I wouldn't be caught. Soon I heard him snoring in a slow rhythm, so I made my way down the stairs to the back door.

As I pulled the door open, a torrent of rain and blowing leaves hit me in the face and splattered across the floor. I drew in my breath and ducked my head into the wind as I stepped out of the doorway. Our backyard was as full of water as the Powderhorn, and it was not until I felt grass and mud oozing between my toes that I realized I had forgotten to put on my shoes. There was no point in going back for them now, though. Anyway they were too wet to wear after my swim in the bayou. I ran barefoot through the wind and rain to the church. The wind knocked me to my knees once, but I made it at last to the church doors. I pulled on the latch, but the doors were locked. Papa never locks the church, so I knew it must have been Sissy Weed who had locked the doors from the inside.

I banged on the door, trying to make her hear me, and all the while getting every bit as soaked as I had been earlier. I didn't know how I was going to explain it to Mama one more time.

"Sissy! Sissy Weed!" I called, as I knocked on the doors, risking that Mama and Papa would hear me. It was a small risk, though, because I could hardly hear my own voice above the sound of the storm.

Lightning made fire flowers in the sky and the thunder boomed in response to my cry.

"Damn this storm!" I said, shaking my fist at the heavens.

It must have shocked the Lord to hear me swearing like Shakespeare because the storm hit a lull for a moment, just like the Almighty was sucking in his breath in shock and amazement. Never let it be said that I don't take advantage of opportunity when it's handed to me, because I used the lull to bang on the door and call Sissy's name once more.

She heard me this time and opened the door just as the storm rallied its strength again. Water inside the church was up to my ankles and well-nigh up to midcalf on little Sissy Weed. Rain was still coming in by the bucketsful through the hole in the roof.

"Lordy if it doesn't look like Noah's flood in here. Come on, we've got to get you to a dry spot," I said, taking Sissy's hand. I pulled her close to me and wrapped part of my cloak around her. Though why I did that, I don't know. The cloak was as wet as the weather. But that didn't bother Sissy Weed any. She clung to me like honeysuckle to the fence post. Together we headed out into the storm again.

Sissy, small and frail as she is, proved a big help to me in getting the kitchen door closed again, once we got inside. She even helped me mop up the leaves and water that blew in. Maybe she realized that it was important that I not leave any traces of what I had done to be found the next morning.

We made it up the stairs and into my room without rousing Mama and Papa, but that didn't mean all of my problems were solved. There was now the problem of what to do with our wet clothes, not to mention what to do with Sissy.

She stood looking at me, wide-eyed and trusting, like she was sure I would know what to do. I couldn't let her down, and when I noticed she was shivering, that at least gave me a place to start.

"Let's get out of these wet clothes," I whispered. From my wardrobe, I took two of my nightgowns and handed one to Sissy. She took it in her hands, but stared at it curiously, not knowing what to do with it.

"Take the wet clothes off," I said and showed her what I meant by stripping down to my skin. I used a quilt from my bed to dry myself, then pulled the dry nightgown over my head. Sissy got the idea and stripped down and dried herself, too. I was shocked to see that she wore no underwear beneath the shapeless smock she had acquired from the Seamores. But I had little time to worry about it, because I had to think of something to do with the soggy mass of clothing we'd left on the floor. I shoved it all under my bed, a place that, over the years, has served to hide many of my transgressions.

My next problem was Sissy. Looking around my

room, my eyes fell upon the wardrobe again. It was big and roomy, with a base big enough for a tiny person to sleep curled up. Unlike Lilly Downs's, the bottom of my wardrobe was not full of shoes. I had only one pair which I'd gotten wet, and which Mama now had sitting under the kitchen table.

"Here," I said, pulling another quilt from my bed. "We'll make you a pallet."

I folded the quilt into a sort of mattress on the floor of the wardrobe and gave her my rabbit fur muff to use as a pillow. I had to crawl in myself to demonstrate to her that I meant for her to sleep there, but she got the idea soon enough.

Leaving the door ajar so she would have air inside, I slipped into my own bed and fell asleep at last.

One of Pharaoh's generals shouted at his army, forcing them to ride their mounts into the sea in hot pursuit of the Children of Israel. But the Egyptians were mounted on camels, and the camels balked because the sea wouldn't part for them as it had done for the Israelites. The camels got so mad they spat a stream of hellfire at the general, and that made him shout even louder.

I opened my eyes and stared at the ceiling in my room. I wished that general would stop all his hollering. Slowly it dawned on me that it wasn't Pharaoh's general making all the racket, but one of Uncle Sam's sergeants. So fogged was my mind after my night in the rain, it took a while longer to realize that it wasn't the Red Sea and the Israelites the soldiers were concerned with, but Smugglers' Cove and Sissy Weed.

I jumped out of bed and ran to my wardrobe quicker than a scared rabbit. Sissy lay on the folded quilt sleeping peaceful as ever you please. She must have been even more tired than I was after our day in the storm.

A sound in the hallway outside my door startled me, but I gathered my wits quickly enough to close the wardrobe door and jump back into bed. I pretended to be just opening my eyes as Mama slowly opened my door and peeked inside.

"Are you awake, Dear?" she asked.

"Yes, Mama," I said, trying to sound groggy.

"You've slept so late. Did the storm keep you awake?"

"Only for awhile."

"Well, get dressed and come on down to breakfast. Papa's already eaten and gone over to meet with the Board of Deacons about the storm damage to the church."

"Oh, I can't eat!"

"You can't? Why not?"

"I mean I can't eat downstairs. I can't go down there." I tried not to let my eyes wander to the wardrobe.

"And why can't you go downstairs?" Mama asked, beginning to sound a little annoyed.

"Because . . . Because I think I have . . . cholera."

"Cholera? Really?" Mama asked.

"But it's not the serious kind," I said quickly, realizing I'd made a mistake by borrowing from R. J.'s imagination.

Mama stepped over to my bed and put her hand on my forehead. "What makes you think it's not the serious kind?" she asked, using the tone of voice she uses with the grocer when she thinks he's charging too much for eggs.

"Well, I think it's the kind that only gives you a little sore throat and a cough. You know what I mean. That kind. Not serious."

"I see," she said. "Perhaps we should have a second opinion. Should I send for Doctor Teague?"

"Oh no!"

"No, I thought not," she said, starting for the door. "By the way," she said turning back to me. "Mrs. Seamore's charm and deportment class has been canceled today."

I hadn't even thought of charm and deportment class. If I had, I would have only worried about what to do with Sissy while I was gone. And as I thought of Sissy, I realized that she would be waking soon and she would probably be hungry. I had to think of some way to get her some food.

"I'm a mite hungry, Mama," I said.

"Do I take that as a sign you are feeling better? Remarkable recovery."

"It's not what you think, Mama. I really do feel better."

"I'm sure you do. And fortunately you didn't take the news about charm and deportment class too hard. There's some breakfast on the stove," she said turning to the door again. "I'll be in my sewing room working on my quilt."

As soon as I heard Mama's footsteps on the stairs, I hurried to my wardrobe and flung open the door.

"You'd better get out and stretch your bones," I said, reaching for Sissy's hand.

She looked around my room as if it was the most curious sight she'd ever seen. After she'd stood up awhile, I had her get back in the wardrobe while I went downstairs. I didn't want to risk Mama coming upstairs again and finding her.

I ate a little of the oatmeal Mama had made, and put the rest in a bowl for Sissy. I found a pan of biscuits left over from the night before and two pieces of fried ham. I took those up for Sissy, too.

"You know, I can't keep you caged up in that wardrobe all the time," I said to Sissy when she had finished eating.

She pointed to the window and said something to me in the unknown tongue.

"Are you talking about leaving? I asked. "Where would you go?"

She said something in reply.

"Where ever you go, you'll be caught and whipped. Maybe hanged."

Again, she said something in reply. It was a strange conversation we were having, each talking in her turn, and neither of us knowing what the other was saying.

If I could just get her to safety. But where was safety? The northern states? That was half a continent away. She was sure to be caught before she reached there. Mexico! Travis Lassiter had said there was no slavery there, and it was certainly closer than the northern states. Of course that was no sure bet either. The Brazoria County slaves had been hanged before they even got started. I'd have to think of a foolproof plan. But before I got much thinking done, I heard Mama coming up the stairs again, and I had to shove Sissy into the wardrobe.

Mama stuck her head in the doorway. "Sarah . . ." She wrinkled up her nose in a strange way.

"What is it, Mama?"

"You know, I think I smell mildew. At least something damp. Do you think the roof could have leaked and got something in your wardrobe wet?"

"I don't think so."

"I'll just have a look." She started for the wardrobe.

"Mama!"

"What is it?" She asked turning quickly back to me with an alarmed expression on her face.

"It's . . . it's nothing. I mean nothing's wet in there. I just looked."

"Well there's *something* damp in here," she said, sniffing the air again.

I remembered the wet clothes I had shoved under my bed after I brought Sissy in from the storm.

"It smells damp everywhere after the storm last night," I said. "Things will dry out eventually."

"I should hope so," she said, shaking her head. "Oh, I almost forgot why I came up. You have a visitor. R. J. is here."

"R. J.!"

I could hardly contain my excitement. With his imagination, he'd be certain to come up with something to do about Sissy.

"You act as if you hadn't seen him in a year," Mama said as she walked downstairs with me.

"Do I? I can't imagine why you'd think that."

"The way the two of you are always running off to the bayou to fish, and you getting in scrapes with boys. I don't know, Sarah, I just thought that by now you'd be more interested in — "

"By jingo you took long enough to get down here!" R. J. said when I stepped into the parlor.

Mama flinched and paled a little at the slang expression R. J. used, but she didn't scold him. She just smiled and said she'd be in the sewing room working on her quilt.

"You look terrible," R. J. said, looking at my hair, which I hadn't gotten around to braiding yet.

"You'd look terrible too if you had spent the night in a hurricane."

"Warn't no hurricane. Just a storm."

"It was close enough."

"I know somebody else who spent the night out in the storm."

"R. J., you can tell me later. I have something important — "

"It was that new slave gal. The one they call Sissy.

108

The mayor and the soldiers never found her. They even think she might have drowned."

"R. J. — "

"The way they figure it, she probably tried to row out to sea. Sam Bradley's rowboat was missing. I figure she took it."

"R. J. — "

"Nobody could have kept a rowboat upright in those swells last night. And of course, the mayor's fit to be tied! 'Cause even if they find her, a dead slave won't be worth nothing to him."

"She's here!" I whispered.

"Who?"

"Sissy."

"You found her body?" R. J. asked, wide-eyed.

"No, silly. She's alive, and she's upstairs in my wardrobe closet."

"You've gone plumb crazy from being out in a hurricane."

"I'm not crazy. I found her on the beach last night, and I'm hiding her in my room. And we're both lucky to be alive. The Widow Watson tried to drown us."

"Lying's a mortal sin, Sadie."

"I'm not lying. Don't you dare accuse me of it, and don't call me Sadie!"

"Sarah, I know you couldn't have found Sissy out on the beach and brought her home and paraded her in front of your folks just to put her in your wardrobe closet. Besides, your Mama told me when she let me in just a minute ago, that you was alone when you came in looking like a drowned rat last night. She made a point of telling me you was alone, because she thought all the time you was with me. And she didn't say a word about the Widow Watson trying to kill you."

R. J. can be very tiring. I had to start from the beginning and tell him how I had happened to find Sissy, how I'd seen the widow and how I'd hid Sissy in the church. I told him everything, all the way up to where I fed Sissy breakfast.

"What are you going to do now?" R. J. asked, without even apologizing for calling me a liar, although he obviously knew by now that I wasn't one.

"That's where I need your help," I said. "You've got to help me think of a way to get her to safety."

"Mexico," he said. "We could send her to Mexico."

"I've already thought of that, but how? Remember the Brazoria County slaves were hanged, along with the white man who tried to help them."

"Oh Lordy!" R. J. said, sounding desperate. "I can't think of a thing."

"Where's that imagination of yours?"

"Now don't get cross with me," he said, getting up to leave. "I'll just have to study on it."

"Well, you haven't got much time to study on it. She can't stay locked up in my wardrobe forever." I found myself talking to R. J.'s back as he let himself out our front door.

I walked by Mama's sewing room before I started upstairs, just to satisfy myself that she hadn't overheard any of our conversation. My heart did a *flip-flop* when I saw that she wasn't in there. I raced up the stairs and found her in my room. She turned to me with her hands on her hips and *that* look on her face. My breath caught in my throat, and I felt sure my sudden dizziness meant my blood had frozen in my veins.

"Young lady, I'm not happy with you."

I could do nothing but stare at her, waiting.

"What is the meaning of this?" she asked.

Relief washed over me. She was pointing to the mass of soggy clothes she had pulled from under my bed. Sissy's dress was crumpled under my nightgown, so Mama hadn't noticed it.

"I said, what is the meaning of this? These clothes were under your bed. They're already beginning to turn sour. I *knew* I smelled something. Now tell me. What is the meaning of this?" Her eyes were shooting sparks, and the sound of her voice was as sharp as a blade.

"I . . . I went out in the storm again last night," I said, not wanting to lie to her.

"Why?"

"Because I . . . I heard the shingles from the church tearing away in the storm, and I . . . I wanted to see if anything got wet." I prayed silently that I wouldn't have to explain any further.

"And you threw your wet nightgown under the bed?"

"Yes, Ma'am."

"But that doesn't explain this," she said, holding up Sissy's soggy, shapeless dress.

She had seen it after all! I couldn't think of a thing to say.

"Sarah, I insist that you tell me where this came from."

"I can't," I whispered.

"You what?"

"I can't."

"You mean you won't."

"Yes," I said near tears. "I won't."

The look on Mama's face changed from anger to hurt.

"Sarah, I've never known you to be this way." Her voice was almost pleading, and I feared she was going to cry. I hated hurting her, but the stakes were higher for Sissy. I feared that if I told anyone at all — even Mama — about Sissy, she would suffer more than hurt feelings. She could be killed.

Mama looked at me for a long time with the hurt

expression on her face. "Very well," she said after a time. "You stay in your room for awhile. Maybe you'll decide to tell your father the truth." She turned and left my room abruptly, taking the wet clothing with her.

I'd seen the tears about to spill from her eyes before she left. She wouldn't be back in my room until Papa got back to the house, I knew. I let Sissy out of the wardrobe to stretch again, but I didn't say anything to her. I felt lower than the belly of a snake.

Sissy looked worried, too. I'm sure we'd have both gone clean out of our minds with nothing to do but sit and stare at each other all day. As it happened, we didn't have to. Papa finished looking over the damage to the church and was back in the house in less than an hour, and Mama sent him up to see me.

He walked into my room looking somber, just like he does when he preaches a funeral. "What's this your mother tells me about your keeping things from her?" he asked.

"I'm sorry to be a worrisome burden," I said.

"Well, it is truly a burden when your mother has reason to believe you've turned to theft."

"Theft?" At first I was confused, until I realized Mama must have thought I stole that dress Sissy had been wearing. "Oh no," I said. "I've never stolen a thing in my life." *Why,* I wondered, *would she think I'd want to steal an ugly thing like that?*

"I'm right glad to hear that," Papa said. "But now you must tell me where this . . . this frock in question . . . came from."

Papa looked at me, waiting for an answer, but once again, words failed me.

"Sarah — " he sounded impatient.

"I can't tell you, Papa."

"What?"

"Please don't ask me anymore."

He stood and took a step toward me. "I'll have none of this, Sarah," he said. "You must — " He stopped speaking and turned to look at the wardrobe.

I had heard it, too — a tiny muffled sound, like a kitten sneezing.

Papa moved like a Pharisee walking through the temple. In two long strides he was in front of the wardrobe. He opened the door, and his eyes fell upon the sacrifice.

Sissy, still wearing the nightgown I had loaned her, was no longer huddled in the corner, but stood straight and tall in the middle of the wardrobe, with my frocks hanging behind her like curtains behind an altar.

She took a step down to the floor, not with the stumbling you might expect from a sacrificial lamb, but with the grace of a princess. She stood right up to Papa and looked him in the eye, waiting.

It's a strange sight to see a minister with nothing to say, but Papa just stood there with his mouth open and speechless. He looked first at Sissy and then at me, wearing a look of confusion.

"Papa, this is Sissy Weed," I said, sounding as if I was introducing a new playmate.

Papa's expression changed suddenly from confusion to dread. "Is she . . . ?"

I nodded my head slowly.

"May the Lord help us all," Papa said, stumbling backward to the bed and collapsing upon it, his shoulders slumped with the burden of truth that had just descended upon him like a black dove.

Mama stepped into my room just then, taking the entire scene in with a glance. She went to Papa's side, sat beside him and picked up one of his hands, patting it gently.

"You will explain?" Papa asked in a weak voice.

"The Seamores whipped her for dropping the lemonade, and she ran away."

"I know that part."

"She is African, brought here illegally. She shouldn't even be here."

"I guessed that much. I want to know how she got in your room."

"I found her."

"You found her?" Papa asked amazed. "But how could you find her when all those soldiers couldn't find her?"

"Out by the cove, wasn't it?" Mama said. "That's what you were doing out in the storm. But how did . . . ?"

I told them the whole story, beginning with the contraband slaves being unloaded from the ship, up to bringing her in from the church during the storm and hiding her in my wardrobe. I didn't leave out the part about how I knew Sissy thought the captain was a murderer, and neither did I leave out the part about the widow at the bridge during the storm. Sissy's eyes never left me as I spoke, and once again I had the feeling that she knew everything I was saying without being able to understand the words.

"A fine mess!" Papa said, standing up to pace the floor and rubbing his hands together. "Are you certain that was the Widow Watson you saw out by the bridge?"

"Quite sure, Papa."

"A fine mess, indeed," he said. "But there's nothing to do but to turn her over to the Seamores."

"Oh no! We can't do that," I cried.

"But it's the law," Papa said firmly. "We must obey the law."

115

"Even when the law isn't right?" I asked.

Papa looked at me for a moment without answering. I'd made him angry, I knew. As if to confirm it, he doubled up his fist and hit my wardrobe. Sissy looked frightened, and Mama and I were both shocked; we'd never seen him act like that before. It didn't hurt my wardrobe much, but it sure skinned Papa's hand. He walked out of my room, cradling his wounded hand and moaning slightly.

"We'd best leave him alone," Mama whispered, still a little awed. I agreed silently. I wasn't about to do anything to make him any more angry than he already was. Mama took a long look at Sissy. "We ought to get you properly dressed," she said, as if to get her mind off Papa's anger. She rummaged through my wardrobe closet until she found a dress I had outgrown. Then she found some pantaloons and a petticoat.

Sissy seemed to enjoy dressing in my outgrown clothes, and Mama and I were having a fine time too, forgetting for a moment the real dilemma. I had just gone to my ribbon box and pulled out a lavender strip of satin to tie in the tight wiry curls of Sissy's hair when Papa knocked softly on the door.

"Come in, Papa," I said.

He stepped inside and gave Sissy and me a long look.

"I have been in great agony," he said at last.

"I'm sorry to cause you agony, Papa," I said.

"It's not your doing. You've only made me see what I must do. I've known in my heart all along that this slavery, this owning another human being, is wrong, but I've lacked the courage to speak out against it. There are some powerful men who argue that these people are better off being cared for by their masters. I knew all along, of course, that only cattle and horses are better off being owned and cared for. But I've been afraid, because disa-

116

greeing seems to threaten to split not only churches, but the whole nation."

"You're brave, Bill," Mama said, going to him.

"No, Sarah's the brave one. A little child shall lead us."

I felt both proud and relieved. Now that Papa was admitting he felt the same way I did, I felt sure he would take over and find a way to get Sissy to safety.

"How will you do it?" I asked. "How will you get her to freedom? Is there a safe way for us to get her to Mexico without . . ."

"Sarah, I said before, the child will have to be turned over to the Seamores." Papa placed his hand gently on Sissy's head as he spoke.

"But, Papa!"

"I'm sorry, but there's nothing else to do. We could try to get her to the North, but the risks are great if she's caught. And she's just a child. She couldn't make it on her own."

"But the Seamores whipped her! They'll — "

"I told you before, we must obey the law. And there's still the matter of the dead man who was found on the bayou. If there is anything to what you believe this black child is saying about Captain Reed, then the sheriff should know about it. Are you sure this . . . this Arab I contracted for with the army knows the African language?"

"He says he does."

"Very well. I'll find him and we'll go to the sheriff. But we still can't keep the fact that we've found the child from the Seamores. They still have every legal right to her. But I'll talk to them about moral rights. That's all I can do. We can only leave her in the hands of the Lord after that."

"Papa, what will you say to the Seamores? Will you

117

tell them that it's wrong for one person to own another? Because that's the truth! It is wrong!"

"I know. I know. But sometimes the truth is too much to take all at once. We have to give it to people in little doses until they've finally accepted the whole amount. But yes, I'll tell them that I believe it's wrong. I'll give them the first dose."

He smiled sadly as he said that and stood up as if to leave.

"Wait, Papa," I called. "Do you . . . do you have to tell them right away that I've found her?"

"Putting it off will only make matters worse," he said. "But I will agree to go to the sheriff's office. We'll leave it up to the sheriff to send for the Arab as well as for the Seamores."

When he had gone, Mama gave Sissy and me each a hug. "You're quite a lady," she said to me, "and maybe I never understood what a true lady is before." She left the room too, wiping her eyes with the corner of her apron.

Sissy and Papa and I were waiting in the sheriff's office when His Honor the Mayor and Mrs. Seamore arrived. The mayor was fairly frothing at the mouth with excitement when he got to the sheriff's office. Mrs. Seamore was all in a dither as well.

"The McCluster girl found her, you say?" the mayor asked as he stepped in the door, then he caught sight of me. "What a brave young lady you are," he said smiling and patting me on the head. You've outdone the United States Army. We'll see that you're rewarded, won't we my dear?" he said, turning to Mrs. Seamore.

Mrs. Seamore had been glaring at Sissy Weed who was sitting huddled in the corner looking frightened and betrayed. And me being the betrayer, I couldn't bear to look at her.

"A reward indeed," Mrs. Seamore said when the

mayor had gotten her attention. "Miss Sarah has always been my star pupil in charm and deportment classes, and I think I know just the reward for her. I happen to know she needs a new thimble."

I was about to tell her she could keep her thimbles when Hi Jolly walked in and saved me from embarrassing myself. He took everything in with one glance around the room.

"That is the African child whose words you wish me to interpret?" he asked, pointing to Sissy.

"That's her," the sheriff said.

"Now just a minute," His Honor said. "What's going on here?"

"Miss Sarah seems to think this girl knows who killed the man we found dead on the bayou, and this Arab here can interpret what she says," the sheriff explained.

"That pickaninny has nothing to say. She's my property and she has nothing to say," the mayor said, growing agitated.

"Now, Mayor, let's just see what turns up," the sheriff said in a calm voice. "If there's going to be a clue here to what happened to that poor feller we found on the bayou, the least I can do is listen." He nodded his head to Hi Jolly, indicating that he was to speak to Sissy.

Hi Jolly walked up to Sissy and spoke to her in words that sounded like a distant drumbeat, and Sissy answered with the same dancing rhythm. Their exchange went on for several minutes until Hi Jolly turned to the sheriff and said, "She says a ship's captain killed a man because he saw him unloading her people from his ship. She said the man argued with the captain and with a woman for awhile, but the captain hit him with the butt end of his pistol, then dragged his body to the bayou. She

119

said the captain is the same man who was at her master's party last evening."

"That's preposterous," the mayor said. "Captain Reed knew she was accusing him of something. She thought he was an evil spirit or something. You know how superstitious these people are."

"I'd like to question Captain Reed," the sheriff said.

"Are you taking the word of a slave?" His Honor asked, sounding indignant. "You know she probably made the whole thing up."

"She didn't make up the dead man I found on the bayou that morning I was chasin' camels. How did she know about that?" Sheriff Duncan asked.

His Honor fussed and fumed for awhile, saying how he didn't like his guests insulted and how you couldn't trust slaves to ever tell the truth and how Sheriff Duncan was going to remember this when the next election came up.

"Now, Mayor," Sheriff Duncan said. "You know I got to do my duty and follow through on this."

Maybe he did his duty; I can't say. I just know nothing much changed. When the sheriff went looking for Captain Reed, he found his ship had sailed as soon as the storm ended, and it seems the Widow Watson went with him. Mr. Lassiter asked him if he was going to send a message on the telegraph to Galveston, to see if Captain Reed showed up there. But Sheriff Duncan said he didn't believe he'd bother, since it was just a little slave girl who was accusing him. Nobody would put any stock in her words, he said.

Even Papa's life was not much different. He still couldn't get rid of his great agony. He had tried to convince the Seamores of the wrong they were doing by owning slaves, and instead of threatening to pull out of the church and take half the congregation with them as Papa feared they would, His Honor told Papa he'd double his contribution to the offering plate if he'd just not bother him with his views.

But worst of all, nothing changed for Sissy. She went back to the Seamores. Lilly Downs said she heard she got another whipping. So much for leaving things in the hands of the Lord. At least, *sometimes*.

I had my own great agony worrying about Sissy and wondering if what Lily said was true. There wasn't much I could do to get my mind off of it either. I didn't even have charm and deportment class to go to anymore.

Mama and Papa said I couldn't learn to conduct myself with charm and good deportment in an atmosphere of inhumanity. What they meant of course, is that they thought the Seamores were setting a bad example by owning slaves. I guess they finally realized that I could pick up worse habits from the Seamores than I could from my friend R. J.

I would walk by the Seamores' house now and then to try to get a glimpse of Sissy Weed, but I never did. I thought of knocking on the door and inquiring about her, but I didn't think it would do any good. Besides, Mama and Papa had forbade me to go inside the house or even on the grounds.

The day I got the message from Bella, though, I disobeyed. The message came through R. J. He had been to the Seamores' house to deliver some vegetables his mama had grown in her garden, and was selling to the

Seamores. Bella was the one who took his delivery, and she told R. J. to tell me something.

"She said to tell you she found your thimble and you're to come get it," R. J. said.

I was so stunned I didn't think I'd heard him right, and I had to ask him to repeat it.

"That's what she said all right," he said. "I told her I'd be glad to take the thimble to you since I see you most every day, but she wouldn't hear of it. Said you had to come get it yourself. She said you were to come just after sundown."

Bella couldn't have found my thimble. It was still at home, safe in my sewing box, and I suspected Bella knew that all along. There had to be some reason why she wanted to see me. At sundown, I walked up to the Seamores' back fence. In a little while Bella came out with a bucket full of chicken feed and started strewing it around on the ground for the chickens, slowly inching her way over to the fence.

"Miss Sarah, I knew you'd come," she said without looking at me. She was surrounded by white Leghorns clucking contentedly as they pecked at the grain she sifted through her fingers to the ground.

"What's this about my thimble?"

"Hush, child. It ain't your thimble I want to talk about. It's that Sissy Weed."

"What about her? Is she all right? Is she . . ."

"I don't want to see that child whipped no more. I done seen enough. But Miz Seamore ain't goin' to stop. You got to help her, Miss Sarah."

"I want to help her, Bella. What can I do?"

"You got to get her away from here. You tried to help her once. I done heard all about it, so I know I can trust you. And I'll help you."

"But how? What — "

At just that moment, Mrs. Seamore stuck her head out the back door and yelled, "Bella, where are you? I told you to send Sissy to me. Why won't she obey? Am I going to have to whip her again?"

"You'll think of something, Miss Sarah. I knows you will," Bella said as she hurried away.

You'll think of something. Didn't Bella know I had been trying to think of something ever since I had found Sissy in the storm? And R. J. had too. He had come up with a wild and impractical scheme for her to be a stowaway on a ship. Only he never could figure out how to get her aboard without being caught. Or how, if he did get her aboard, he could make sure something terrible didn't happen to her if she was discovered after the ship sailed.

I went out of my way to go by R. J.'s house before I went home. I told him what Bella had said, then I went home and spent a sleepless night wondering what we could do. By morning I still couldn't think of a thing. *Where were miracles when you needed them?*

That afternoon, I paced the floor in my room still trying to think of something, and as I did, I looked down from my window and saw what I took to be a miracle walking up our front steps. It was R. J. He had no doubt put that magnificent imagination of his to work and had come up with some way to help Sissy Weed. I ran to my window and leaned over the ledge to call to him.

"R. J.! I knew you'd come up with something. I'll be right down and you can tell me what it is."

I raced downstairs, opened the front door and ran smack into R. J., near about knocking him over.

"I've got some good news," he said.

"I knew it! What is it?"

"I got you a camel ride."

"What?"

"A camel ride. You been wanting one for a year. Ever

since the army first brought them critters in. Hi Jolly and Mendez finally got the last of the camels rounded up, and the sergeant in charge of the troops here gave Hi Jolly permission to give the kids in town one last ride before all the camels leave.

He had clean forgotten about Sissy. Drat that Frenchman!

"R. J., what about . . ." Since we were standing outdoors, I feared someone would hear me. I leaned close and whispered, "What about you know who?"

"What? Oh, you mean . . . Oh, well . . . I haven't come up with a thing. Just give me a little more time. But how about that camel ride? Hi Jolly's waiting."

I swear, I was mad enough to hit him. But I showed great restraint.

"Don't bother me with camel rides, you nincompoop!" I said and slammed the door in his face.

I had just turned around to go back upstairs when an idea struck me like a tongue of fire at Pentecost.

I flung the door open, hoping R. J. hadn't gone yet, and there he was, still on the front steps, rubbing his nose where the hastily slammed door had hit him.

"When can I have that camel ride?" I asked.

"What? But you just said — "

"Never mind what I just said. When can I have the camel ride?"

"You promise you won't hit my nose again?"

"Yes, I promise. Now tell me."

"Hi Jolly said it would have to be today. The sergeant says he wants to start moving the camels out tomorrow."

"Today? Then there's not much time. Tell him I'll . . . wait a minute. R. J. come inside and wait for me. I want to write notes to Hi Jolly and Mendez. Will you deliver them for me?"

"Sure, but I don't see why you — "

"Hush, R. J. You'll see soon enough."

I sat down at Papa's writing desk in the parlor and used some of his paper and ink. R. J. stood behind me, reading over my shoulder as I wrote.

"Oh Lordy!" he said as he read.

I blew on the paper to dry the ink, then folded it and handed it to R. J.

"Get going!" I said.

He hurried out the front door and I ran upstairs to get to work.

There wasn't much time to get together everything I needed for the camel ride. I had to find my pink gingham bonnet, the one Mama always wants me to wear in the summer, because it covers my face and keeps me from getting more freckles. I also had to sew up the hole in the thumb of my white gloves. My shoes were becoming stiff and cracked as a result of the dunking in the bayou, but I'd softened them up as well as I could with grease. I packed a quick lunch in our picnic basket. Papa had given me a little money to save until the dry goods peddler came down from Houston again. Papa said I was to use the money to buy shoes from him. But I would need that money now, so I took it from my trinket box.

I knew Mama was busy in her sewing room, and Papa was over at the church working on a sermon. I didn't see any use in bothering them, so I just took all the things I had gathered and went to meet R. J.

Under the guise of peddling vegetables, the two of us went to the Seamores' back door. Bella answered our knock, and we had to talk fast to explain the plan to her. Without a word, she took the basket from us and went back into the house. R. J. went his way, and I hurried home and up to my room.

It was just before sundown. Papa was still over at the

126

church and Mama was still in her sewing room, and I sat in my room watching the street from my window. In a little while I saw R. J. walking along the street. It looked like Sarah McCluster in a pink gingham dress, white gloves and a bonnet that covered her face was walking along with him.

My plan was to stay in my room, because it wouldn't do for people to see *two* of me out on the streets.

But I am possessed with a great curiosity, as well as a lack of resistance to certain temptations. And the temptations to watch R. J. and the daughter of the Reverend and Mrs. McCluster as they made their way to the bayou, was too much for me. I followed along behind, hiding in bushes and dusky shadows.

My heart jumped when they met Willie Barlow and his mama on the sidewalk. But R. J. just nodded his head in a polite greeting to Mrs. Barlow and "Sarah" kept her head down so the bonnet would hide her black face. It worked well enough, because I saw from my hiding place in the shadows that Willie turned around and stuck his tongue out at "Sarah's" back.

After we left the street on which the church and parsonage are located, I had to run down an alley to keep from being seen. Then, once I reached the edge of town, I hid behind clumps of brush and small trees as often as I could. I was taking a great risk I knew, but it was important to me to see firsthand that my hastily made plan was going to work.

As we neared the bayou, I saw that a few more pieces of my plan had fallen into place. There were *two* Hi Jollies there, just as I had arranged. R. J. and "Sarah," and a camel, were also standing nearby. No one else was around because Hi Jolly had done as I asked and sent all the other camel riders home.

I saw R. J. walk up to one of the Hi Jollies. It was

really Mendez, wearing a turban belonging to the real Hi Jolly, but from a distance you couldn't tell them apart. R. J. handed Mendez a packet, and I knew it was the money I had taken from the box I kept under my bed. He would need it more than I needed high button shoes. Then the real Hi Jolly tapped the camel's knees, making him kneel. He reached for "Sarah's" hand to help her into the saddle, but before she took his hand, she turned and looked in the direction where I was hiding behind a small bush.

She broke loose and ran toward me. I could see tears glistening in her eyes as she said, "Si Si Wee, thank you, please." She flung her thin arms around my neck. For a few minutes, we hung onto each other like we were long lost cousins, then Sissy Weed ran back to the waiting camel.

When she was in the saddle, Mendez, dressed as Hi Jolly, got the beast to its feet and led it toward the south. They would have to pass along one edge of town where it was likely people could look out their windows and see Hi Jolly giving Sarah McCluster that camel ride she'd wanted for so long.

"Mendez says he'll see she gets to his family in Mexico," R. J. said, joining me.

"The he cimmel will be the best way for crossing the Mexican desert," Hi Jolly said, smiling, "and the girl will be safe because she is with the best cimmel man in the whole world . . . almost."

I watched Sissy Weed disappearing over the horizon on her ship of the desert, and as I watched, I went over in my mind how I was going to tell Papa and the Lord that there are some things you just have to take into your own hands.